# MAGIC FIRE

## SEDONA VENEZ

# WANT FREE SEDONA VENEZ BOOKS?

Sign up for Sedona Venez's Newsletter and receive FREE BOOKS. In addition to the free stories, you will also get special pricing, exclusive previews and news of new releases.

**GET A FREE SEDONA VENEZ BOOK!**

Join Sedona's mailing list to be the first to know of new releases, free books, special prices and other author giveaways.

https://sedonavenez.com/free-book

❦  I  ❦

ALL THE DREAMERS want to make their way to New York City, chasing the bright lights, and the even brighter lives that they imagine are waiting for them, in the concrete jungle and grit. They flood in, year after year, ready to take the world by storm. I saw it *all* the time. I saw the hope, the wonder, the naïve anticipation that this was where they were supposed to be.

And for some of them, they were right on the money. Most, however, would join the mass exodus back to wherever they hailed from, poor and broken, but not defeated. That's what I admired so much about humans: the resilience of their spirit. They put up with all the bullshit a city like New York had to offer. It chewed them up and spit them out, but they kept on fighting. They fought for something more, something beyond the mundane that humanity was cursed with. They *never* gave up.

Well. Most of them. The girl that had been sobbing at the bus station outside my apartment building on her cell phone as I walked by on my way to the car, had sounded on the verge of giving up. I couldn't blame her for that. She wanted out. I wanted out, too.

Not forever, of course. Just for the weekend. There was nothing more oppressive to a fae, no matter how pure of blood, than a sprawling metropolis. We did better outside, far from the roar of traffic and shadows of skyscrapers, where we could wriggle our toes in the grass and breathe the clean, crisp air, the natural elements fueling our energies—and our gifts.

Getting out of the city for a weekend was just good practice for health and happiness, honestly. It was why I never missed the gatherings with my sisters; not literal sisters, unfortunately. I was cursed with an older brother, and not a very good one at that. My fae sisters, however, were lifelong companions. The only people in this whole world who understood me completely—and with whom I could be myself entirely. Or at least *most* of them. There were a couple of fae that were barely tolerable at times, but you get those in every group, right?

"Kaye!" I glanced up from my mountain of pillows and blankets to find one of my fae sisters, Catriona, beaming at me from under the tarp I'd mounted over my sleeping arrangements. A gentle breeze fluttered her near-white hair about, looking more like a halo, than anything stereotypically fae. She giggled. "Belladonna and her girls have just arrived! Come say hello!"

I bit my lip to hold back an embarrassing squeal. Sisters had been arriving all evening, and while I wasn't the first to show up that Friday night, my ridiculous need to be early for everything had slotted me amongst the earliest arrivals of the weekend.

It was a twice-yearly event. Fae sisters from all over flocked to our sacred gathering spot within the Appalachians, right on the border of New York and Connecticut. We came to reconnect and rejuvenate our spirits. Nothing was more tiring for a supernatural than being constantly surrounded by humans. Although I made a living working with the most mundane species in the world, I couldn't deny the way they drained me. If I didn't have a chance to meet with my sisters a couple times a year and recharge my batteries, I'd lose my mind.

So, we did the camping thing as a way to get back to nature. Since I'd parked my car in its usual spot and used a bit of magic and fae speed to get far away from the City, my feet hadn't seen the insides of shoes and my dark red waves rolled freely down my back. I had trekked all the way up to our sacred gathering spot in blissful silence, pausing every so often to let the sun wash over me, to absorb the energies from the wind, and to listen to the creatures around me—a far cry from the ceaseless honking cabs, screaming people and wailing sirens I had to deal with back in the city.

We kept our camp hidden from humans—and any other snoops, supernatural or otherwise—with magic, using white gemstones carefully placed across the landscape to channel our wards. Within them, we were free to just be, to exist as we were meant to exist. No magic was off-limits. No more holding back. No more pretending or hiding or downplaying our abilities.

I took Catriona's outstretched hand, and we skipped off together, away from my nest of comfort I would undoubtedly fall into later tonight, drunk on spirits and the love of my sisters. As we hurried through the crowd of hugging, laughing, and chattering fairies, I couldn't help but feel like the dark cloud zooming through a field of sweet pastel flowers. There were stereotypes for a reason, and most of the fae I knew bore the lightness of our kind in their outer appearances. I, meanwhile, tended to wear primarily black clothing that fit snugly around what some might consider generous curves—generous for modern society's ridiculous expectations of women's weight, that is. My hair, while red, was a deep tone of mahogany, rather than fire, and I liked it that way. I had nothing against my sisters embracing the light, but when it came to personal style, I was dark as the night, able to navigate the world in killer heels with equal ease.

*All the while wishing I was barefoot, of course.*

Outsiders may have struggled to grasp how we fit so many bodies on a single campsite, but within our wards, the lands were limitless. Magic was a beautiful thing. It was sad, really, that the laws of this world forbid humans from indulging in it. Any supernatural who was caught willingly sharing their gifts was immediately considered a traitor to their kind. We took all the precautions to make sure no one accidentally stumbled upon our gatherings, and thankfully, the use of wards made it easy. When I glanced up, I could see the shimmer of magic shielding us from the rest of the world. But before that, we left damaged trails in our wake along the mountainside, deterring hikers from taking that path. We erected temporary signs citing prosecution for trespassing on private property. Thus far, we hadn't had a human casualty yet.

We all wanted to keep it that way.

Catriona dragged me through the sea of bodies until suddenly I was throwing myself on Belladonna, making high-pitched, girlish sounds I would never dare utter on a regular day. Today, I just couldn't help myself. Seeing my sisters was life giving. It saved me. It saved us all.

"Kaye, my sweet," Belladonna cooed in my ear, squeezing hard and stroking my hair. "Always my darkest fairy. I've missed you!"

I hugged hard in return, and when we broke apart, our eyes met with shimmering tears in them. My emeralds bore into her honey-browns, adoring her with every fiber of my being.

"I've missed you too," I assured her, beaming so hard my cheeks ached. "We should try to do this more than once a year, Miss Lady, if you can fit me in your bat-shit crazy schedule, that is."

"Oh, honey, I always have time for you!" She pinched my cheek affectionately.

One of the eldest of our sisters, Belladonna traveled the world in a jetsetter lifestyle. She wore lavish clothes and sparkly baubles, yet she was like the den mother when we gathered. Her daughters, Lily and Rose, were shaping up to follow nicely in their mother's footsteps.

I moved onto them next, kissing Lily's milky white cheek and Rose's dusty brown temple. Just a touch revitalized me. We could all feel it. The energy pulsing between us, around us, through us.

"I've been absolutely dying for this weekend," Rose gushed, linking her arm around mine as Lily and Catriona greeted one another. "I don't know what it is about the seasons changing, but I've just about given up on the idea of ever meeting a guy who isn't just interested in sex."

"Something in the summer air makes them dumb as bricks and horny as dogs," Lily agreed with a groan. One of the other reasons we all yearned for these retreats was to escape the men in our lives, human and otherwise. It wasn't their fault, of course, that they pursued us so relentlessly. Fairies attracted men like moths to a flame. Even supernaturals, who had a higher resistance to most magical elements in this world, put us on some ridiculous pedestal. When you're young, it can be flattering. For a year or two, anyway. Then it just gets exhausting. I hadn't dated, courted, or fucked freely in years, mostly because I couldn't handle a man's insane attachment to me after just a couple of dates.

*And because I'd been cut deep, one too many times.* I swallowed down a lump in my throat at the thought, pushing the memories aside.

"I think this is going to be our best gathering yet," Catriona professed, as I threw an arm around Lily's shoulder, dragging her into the conversation with a laugh. Rose and Lily lived up to their names. The wild-child romantic persona fell to Rose with her sumptuous lips and come-hither stare. Lily, meanwhile, was soft and sweet, untouchable and readily wilted if improperly cared for. I loved them both with all my heart. I loved all my sisters, naturally, but there were varying degrees to my affection. The four around me were my nearest and dearest.

"We say that *every* year," Rose replied with a chuckle. "What makes you think this one will be any different?"

Catriona wiggled her dark brows, stark opposite to her white hair, and produced a bottle of fae-brewed wine from her slouchy shoulder bag. We all cheered as she shook it, little flecks of what looked like starlight, dancing inside the bottle. Normally we all drank human-made wine: just as delicious, but not as potent.

"Because good ol' Spirits of the Spry is getting the party started before sundown this time!" Catriona exclaimed, and much to my surprise, the entire gathering joined in on our cheering. "Drink up, ladies!"

I accepted the bottle after Catriona's first sip, taking a swig of the floral-scented liquor. I closed my eyes as Rose took the bottle next, taking a moment to truly feel the liquid trickle down my throat. *Beautiful.* Images of a spring day flashed across my mind—flowers and babbling brooks, and leaves rustling in a cool easterly wind. Already the tips of my fingers tingled, a sip of fae-wine comparable to three full glasses of human-made wine.

And as we took turns sipping from the bottle, I knew that even if this wasn't the best gathering we sisters had ever had, it was *definitely* going to be the rowdiest.

I awoke from a blissful, fae-wine induced slumber to the sound of a deep groan. Not just any groan, mind you. As my eyelashes fluttered, and I inhaled a breath of cool mountain air, the sound reverberated in my bones. A baritone rumble that befitted a god, one that could rattle the mountain range from here to the very ends of the Earth, and back again. When sleep finally left me, I shot up with a sharp gasp, chest heaving as I scanned the area.

Nothing. Catriona lay peacefully beside me, mouth open and drool dribbling onto one of my many, many pillows. Bless the powers that be for magic: there was no way I could have hauled all this crap up here otherwise. One bottomless bag spell and I had a weekend's worth of clothes, pillows, blankets, and booze ready to go.

*Had I dreamed the sound?* My dreams had been fractured, as

they always were. As I blinked the crusty bits out of my eyes, I recalled running, but I couldn't be certain if it was toward something, or away. Shaking my head, I scanned the campsite. Dozens of similar set-ups to mine were spread out over the grounds, full of sleeping fairies, drunk and satisfied after a night of feasting, dancing, and singing around the fire. As I sat up taller, I spied a few of my sisters still awake, sitting by the fire. They spoke in low, harmonious voices. Not one seemed distressed by the sound that echoed through my mind.

I flopped back, harder than I meant to, and rubbed my forehead, groaning. It must have been a dream. It shouldn't surprise me, not after a night of drinking fae-wine.

And yet it happened again. This time I felt the vibrations on the ground, the faint quiver cutting across the earth below and sending a flutter of something through me. I frowned. The vibration... It was like driving over train tracks with your car, taking it just a little too fast and feeling the pleasurable tickle between your thighs.

There one second, gone the next. In a blink of an eye, the groan, now more like a long, lengthy sigh, was gone. As I looked around the sleepy campsite, over the scattered bodies wrapped in silks and homemade quilts, with tarps and awnings strung up magically, attached to the wards and the trees so no sister was blocked out, I scrutinized harder. In the distance, just beyond the fire, it looked as though something had kicked the dirt off.

"Fuck it," I muttered. "This *isn't* a dream."

After grabbing a bathrobe—black, naturally—and cinching the puffy fat belt around my waist, I hesitated, a hand hovering over Catriona. Should I wake her for what could be as silly as me straddling the lines somewhere between dreaming and awake? She'd had a lot more wine than I had, I recalled with a wry grin. I'd probably get a face full of light, followed by mumbled threats of disfigurement if I woke her now, only a few hours after we collapsed onto my pillow fort in a fit of giggles.

Smirking, I padded away and carefully stepped around the

others scattered around me. Careful not to step on toes or fingers or hair, I moved with fae speed—a gift, fleet-footedness and nimble grace—so as not to disturb anyone. My sisters around the fire didn't even look up as I passed, their senses so dulled by wine that they probably wouldn't notice a semi-truck barreling through.

The dust had fluttered at the edge of the camp, between two huge mounds of slate. I pressed a palm to it, trying to feel the vibrations again. Faint, but still present. Eyebrows knitted, I pushed forward, slipping between the stones and following the path higher up the mountainside. I stayed within the wards, of course. Even if it was something more sinister than a too-real dream, it wouldn't be able to pass through our protection charms.

When the path stopped going horizontal and started going vertical, I tightened my bathrobe and took to the climb. Bare feet made for easy climbing, and before I knew it I found myself on a plateau of sorts—right at the mouth of a cave. I glanced over my shoulder, noting the flickering flames of our bonfire in the distance, along with the multi-colored coverings scattered all around it.

Had this cave always been here? We had been coming to this exact spot for years. No one had ever mentioned a cave before, and I swore we had explored every inch of this mountain range at least twice by now.

The hairs on the nape of my neck rose when I took a step toward the dark opening. *A warning.* Turn back. Get out.

"Me and my fucking curiosity," I grumbled. One day, it was going to get me into serious trouble.

Slowly, with practiced purpose, I raised both hands, fingers splayed and palms out, and drew in a deep breath. It came naturally to me now, Illumination. As simple as turning on a light—of any color I chose, at that. When I was a kid, however, trying to get just the tip of my pinky to light up was a challenge, one I'd shed many tears over. Fae were born with a vast wealth of power, but it took time to access it. You had to work for your gifts, apparently.

Nobody ever just opened their mouth and belted a perfect opera aria, I suppose.

I chose a soft, warm yellow light for guidance, in no mood to squint against something obnoxiously bright. Moving on the tips of my toes, I crept along in near silence, sensing now that it wasn't just a noise that had drawn me here, but a presence—one that must have tugged at my subconscious, because I didn't realize it until I was almost totally down the rabbit hole, that I wasn't alone.

Every so often I'd pause, listening, feeling out into the natural world. Yup. There was definitely something here: something inside our wards. Perfect. The little voice at the back of my head insisted that I go back for help, but I pushed forward stubbornly. For the most part, it was just a tunnel into the mountain. Dirty. A little damp. But the air wasn't stale; rather, it had life to it, even as I edged farther from the mouth of the cave.

When I came to yet another mouth, I realized why. As I approached, orange light flickered along the floor and the walls, signaling a fire beyond the opening, so I dimmed my personal light and slowed myself to a crawl, as I peered into the opening.

My jaw dropped before I could stop it. I seemed to have stumbled upon a grand hall of sorts, like the kind dwarves would burrow deep into a mountain's core. The ceiling shot up at least a hundred feet above, revealing an opening from which one could see the stars, beautiful and twinkling and beckoning me forth.

And in the middle of it all, a man sat on a log in front of a healthy fire, roasting something on the end of a stick. I crossed my arms and straightened up, feeling his presence so profoundly and so suddenly that it actually took my breath away—not that I'd let it show, of course. No human could throw me so off-balance, yet he wasn't a supernatural like me.

I inhaled softly. Not like a werewolf breathing in the scent of its prey, but like a snake who flicks its tongue out for just a second to taste the air.

*Shifter.* The word flashed through my mind when his head snapped up, eyes darting in my direction. He must have scented me when I let my guard drop, so startled to find a shifter in our fairy wards that I momentarily forgot myself.

Fuck it. No sense hiding now. We both knew the other was there.

"Hey," he barked, shooting to his feet and marching around his bonfire. Attractive shifter that he was... I couldn't stop myself from skimming his muscular figure, made more prominent by the fact that he was shirtless and totally ripped.

Chestnut brown hair, tousled and thick—begging for someone to run their fingers through and tame it. A chiseled jaw and light eyes: gray, if I wasn't mistaken, and beautiful. Oh, and a six pack that probably made human women weep at first sight, with a tantalizing V-cut guiding my gaze down to the low-hanging waistline of his olive-green sweatpants. Yum. *Yum times a thousand.*

"What are you doing here?" he demanded, handsome face contorted somewhere between surprised and annoyed. I could deal with that. The shifter raised his stick between us, maybe to intimidate, but the now obvious marshmallow on the end was on fire. It bubbled up as I stared at it, my eyebrows shooting up, as it finally fell off and landed on the floor of the cave with an oddly satisfying splat.

I looked up, biting back a grin. "Wow. Terrifying."

"Yeah, well..." He tossed the stick back toward his happy little bonfire. "I don't need a weapon to throw you on your ass. Answer the question."

"No need to be rude, shifter," I fired back, temper prickling at the thinly veiled threat. Arms still crossed, I stepped out of the shadows completely and into the cave, noting the flash surprise, this time surpassing the annoyance that I called him out. Surely he could sense me too. "My sisters and I are camping at the base of the mountain. I..." I swallowed hard. "I couldn't sleep and went wandering. No foul intentions, I swear."

I raised my hands innocently. Lying had never come easily to me, or to most fae. We preferred to play with our words, saying one thing and meaning another, but not outright lying. And this wasn't a lie. Just not the whole truth.

He stood silent for a moment, assessing me, then stepped back, though his body remained tense. "Right. Okay. Not to be rude, I just didn't expect to see other people here."

"Neither did we... inside our shields," I remarked, watching his movements as he made his way back to the log. He moved with the swagger of a confident man, yet there was a slight hunch to his broad, muscular shoulders. "How did you get here?"

"How long have you all been here?" His eyes fixed on the flames as he waited for my response. I took a tentative step forward, then a few more when he didn't react.

"Today."

"Well, I've been out here since Thursday. Must have been caught inside." He glanced up, then swept his gaze up and down my figure. Heat rose to my cheeks—and I was the last person in the world to blush, even in the presence of such a fine specimen. "You a witch?"

I snorted.

"Then what are you?"

"I'm a psychologist from Manhattan," I told him. Most supernaturals were secretive, and with good reason, yet none of my usual fight-or-flight reflexes were kicking in around this shifter. He had a peaceful aura about him—for now. "And my name's Kaye."

"Kaye the fae, huh? Nice."

I laughed again. "So you figured it out?"

Generally, supernatural men were worse than humans when they discovered you were a fairy. For some, our gifts, our pres-ence, our natural beauty—like catnip to the fattest, greediest of cats. Yet the shifter before me gave no indication that it phased him in the slightest. Peculiar.

"It was my first guess, actually," he admitted. When I finally strolled over to the bonfire, he lifted a half-eaten bag of extra-large marshmallows toward me. Smirking, I shoved my hand in and grabbed two—just to be polite. He motioned for me to sit, which I did, but not right away. I took my time, easing around the flames and perching on the far edge of the log. "You have that light about you, I guess. Totally threw me, but I wasn't completely sure."

"Why not?" I popped a marshmallow in my mouth after giving it a subtle sniff. No lingering magic or poisons that I could detect. Tasted like a regular old grocery store marshmallow.

He shot me a crooked grin, one that made my insides twist in ways I wasn't entirely comfortable with. "Well, most of the fairies I know aren't dressed in all black and skulking around in shadows."

"Then you know some pretty boring fairies."

A dark, almost too seductive chuckle followed as he returned his gaze to the flames. "Yeah, I guess that's true."

We sat blanketed in a comfortable silence, him watching the fire and occasionally adding small blocks of wood to it from a pile, me munching on my midnight snack. When I was through, I turned to him, this intriguing shifter with gray eyes and a pleasant, alluring scent.

"And what about you?"

"What about me?"

"You got a name?"

"Sure do."

"And?"

"And I don't just give it to strangers who wander into my vacation cave," he said, smirking. I arched a brow.

"Fair is fair, shifter. I gave you my name." I pursed my lips momentarily. "Or maybe I'll just have to name you myself. Maybe a Calvin or Ewan—"

"Darius," he admitted softly. "I'm a dragon shifter."

I stiffened slightly, then released a breath and willed away the internal prejudice that had built up over the years. There were many kinds of supernatural creatures, yet they seldom interacted with shifters, if they could help it. Even in Alfheim, our underground haven for all things non-human, named after Norse mythology's realm of the elves, supers and shifters tended not to have much to do with one another.

But Darius wasn't looking for an out.

And neither was I.

"So," he said after a few beats, "Kaye the fae is a psychologist, huh? I thought all fairies were, I don't know, poets and dancers and hippies."

"Again, only the boring ones. I bet you think all of us can fly and we're all tiny little things, right? Well, I've never had wings, nor am I remotely skinny," I fired back, biting my tongue about unpleasant shifter stereotypes. Fairies weren't persecuted by the magical communities in the same way that shifters were. They weren't seen as animals, as lesser than. It wouldn't be fair for me to tease him about it when he didn't know me well. "I run a part-time practice with a psychiatrist friend in the city. I love what I do."

He seemed cowed, forcing out a: "Well, good for you."

"And you? What does Darius the Dragon do?" Underwear model. Magazine cover page frequenter. ... Real estate, maybe, with that smile.

"Bodyguard," he said, almost grunting it. "Personal security."

"Really? Who are you protecting out here?"

"My sanity," he offered, this time with a smile. "Everybody needs a few days away."

If I had a drink, I would have toasted him. "I hear that."

Darius lifted the bag again, shaking it. "Want me to make you a s'more?"

I blinked away my disbelief and decided right then and there to just accept the comfort, the feeling that we'd known each other for years, without questioning it. "You bet your ass I do."

I wasn't sure how long we chatted for after, but four s'mores later, the fire burned lower, dropping the hue of the light on the cave walls and harkening me to study the stars overhead. We'd discussed our jobs, our moves to the city, and our need to escape it. Nothing too serious. While alarm bells weren't screaming as I'd inched closer to him on the log, he was still a stranger. A gorgeous stranger, sure, but still a man who hadn't earned access to any of my secrets.

"I can see why you'd come out here," I admitted, head tilted back as I took in the twinkling show of beauty above. An almost perfect circle in the cave's ceiling gave a spectacular view to the night sky. "It's beautiful."

"It really is."

I flinched at the words—Darius almost breathed them in my ear, appearing at my side in a curious silence. Eyes narrowed, I glanced his way and bit back a smile. However, before I could ooze the snarky reply that was bubbling up in my throat, he tucked my hair behind my ear—slowly, carefully, like he was testing the waters. The faintest caress of his fingertips sent a chill down my spine, and I swallowed all my sass as heat bloomed within me.

"I've been fortunate enough to look at something much more beautiful for the last couple hours," he murmured, and even though my immediate reaction was to roll my eyes—which I did, dramatically, paired with a scoff—something inside me squirmed happily at the flattery. Who doesn't want a guy who looks like a sex god complimenting them?

"Wow," I managed, smirking. "You reel in a lot of girls with one-liners like that?"

Darius chuckled, and I stiffened slightly at the feel of his long fingers curving around my wrist. "One or two."

He swallowed my comeback with a kiss, one I fell into almost too willingly. Eyes fluttering closed, I let him pull me into it, our lips finding each other like long lost lovers. The faint tickle of heat within me blossomed to something more scorching, my cheeks prickling with color and my core tightening with desire when Darius nipped gently at my lower lip.

My fingers threaded through his hair as our lips parted, opening to one another with a soft sigh. He grunted in surprise when my tongue swept over his first, and I bit back some sounds of my own when his arm snaked around my waist in response and yanked me closer.

The dragon radiated dominance without coming off as aggressive—the perfect combination, honestly. So, I let myself fall. I let myself succumb, just for a moment, as the dance of our lips, teeth, and tongues grew more complex. Kissing him... It sparked something within me, something I never knew was there before. An inner beast, for lack of a better term, which roared to life the second he pulled away and pressed heated kisses along my jaw and neck.

The creature within demanded sacrifice, appeasement, its hunger for Darius so raw that it frightened me. While I let my head tilt back, knowing his teeth would leave marks on my skin, I had to put a stop to things when I felt him tugging my bathrobe belt loose.

"Wait," I whispered, trying to contain the way my chest heaved, "hold on."

"Sorry, I didn't mean to—"

"It's fine," I said as we broke apart, me righting my clothes and him tucking a pretty noticeable pants-tent out of sight. "I just... I'm not really a one-night stand kind of girl, even with someone as gorgeous as you."

This time I caught the flash of color on his cheeks as he grinned. "Totally understandable. I'm just some dragon you met in a cave."

I took a few steps back, head cocked to the side. "I'm pretty sure there are fairytales out there telling me why that's a bad thing."

"Only if you try to steal my gold." He seemed to want to follow me, moving a half-step after, but then held himself back. "Maybe I could steal your number instead?"

Laughing, I tightened my belt and slowly padded back to the mouth of the cave. "Ask me when the sun comes up, shifter. I'm sure you'll know where to find me."

When the sun comes up and the fae-wine fades, I might have an answer for him. For now, I concentrated on staying upright, giddy from his kiss, and battling the desires of the beast within...

Who wanted nothing more than to run back and mount that beautiful dragon with that sexy smirk, and those steel-gray eyes.

Fae-wine, and one hell of a handsome shifter: a lethal combination, indeed.

$\maltese$ 2 $\maltese$

THIS TIME I didn't wake to the beckoning call of a dragon, riddled with intrigue and mystery, but the dulcet tones of my fae sisters starting off their day. My eyes opened heavily like they were caked in make-up, despite my face being clean, and I rolled over with a groan. At least the awnings overhead kept the sun out, but still, its shimmer managed to pierce through.

Beside me, Catriona was on the exact same wavelength.

"Shut up," she said, moaning. Despite my slight hangover and my lack of sleep, I still managed to smile as I shifted around to face her. My fae sister had been wearing make-up yesterday; mascara smeared across her sinfully pale skin, her under-eye a little puffy. She'd be the talk of the sisters if she didn't clean up. Fairies were noted for their beauty, and anytime you didn't look effortlessly stunning, there were whispers. I was used to it at this point. Slightly rounder in the hip, breast, and butt areas, I'd had fairies gossiping about me since I was a kid, insisting that I wasn't a full fae, that my blood was diluted with human blood— all the usual bullshit that breaks down an already fragile teenage girl's self-esteem.

Luckily I'd gotten past that long ago. Catriona, meanwhile,

was a typical angelic fae, with a crown of near-white hair and dark brows, her features pointed and modelesque. To spare her the ignorant whispers, I shuffled over to my bottomless bag and retrieved an unopened package of make-up remover wipes. Although I would have rather gone back to sleep, I sat up with a languid sigh, stretching to wake my weary limbs, and then cracked open the package and pulled out a wipe.

"What are you doing?" Catriona whined, weakly trying to both push me away and shield her face when I started to clean her up.

"Making you look presentable, my little hungover munchkin," I insisted. "You look like a raccoon."

"And you look like a vampire on good days, so what's the issue?"

I cocked my head to the side, smirking as her eyes fluttered open. There you go. That's how a fae awakens: gently and beautifully.

"I'm gonna chalk that up to the fact you have a hangover and you're just being bitchy," I told her, then shoved the make-up wipe into her hand. Catriona huffed, lower lip pouted out, then sat up with some difficulty.

"Yeah, sorry. I didn't mean it. You don't look like a vampire."

I grinned. "Sometimes I do."

Our eyes met, my emerald greens to her ice blues, and our brief spat, if you could call it that, ended with giggles.

This weekend was my time to get all my giggles out. In the real world, I absolutely was *not* a giggler, but my fae sisters brought it out of me. At least here I wasn't judged. I ran my hands through my hair, which had doubled in size while I slept, full of knots and tangles.

Well, I wasn't judged much.

"Now let me help with that," Catriona offered after I dug out a comb. "Then food. I could really go for a greasy, fatty burger right about now. Or fries. What do those Canadians call that dish with fries and cheese?"

"A poutine?" I replied.

"Yeah, that. I had it once when visiting Montreal, and it was amazing."

"It'll be fae cakes and flowery jams for breakfast, you know that," I muttered, which made her groan. "But maybe I can conjure something that'll appease the Hangover Gods better."

I winced as she dragged the comb through my hair, obviously used to dealing with her straight, relatively thin mane.

"Oh, please! If I don't eat a piece of bacon soon, everyone's going to suffer."

As I watched my sleepy, probably equally hungover fae sisters slowly rise from their sleeping quarters, many looking bleary-eyed but still beautiful, I couldn't help but smile.

"I'll see what I can do."

We'd both need something. Catriona to battle the hangover, me to forget a dragon—otherwise there was no way we'd get through a day of fairy activities with our sisters.

I rubbed my eyes, brushing the crusty bits of sleep out. Ugh. Once I figured out how to conjure a bacon cheeseburger, I'd need a whole pot of coffee to recover from last night—stat. Floral-scented sweet water from the springs of Alfheim was just not going to cut it today.

"Ouch!" I turned my narrowed gaze down to whatever dared embed itself in my foot. Placing a hand on the tree I'd been hiding behind for balance, I lifted my foot and found a thorn, seemingly detached from its prickle bush and just waiting for me to step on it. Tsking, I gripped it firmly and yanked it out.

Heh. Apparently, this weekend was one of fairytales, because last night I had met a dragon in a cave, and now with my lion-like red mane, a thorn had stuck itself in my paw. There had to be a bigger picture here that I was missing.

At the sound of giggles carried on the mid-morning breeze, I ducked down, scanning the terrain. Our gatherings consisted of many things: the days for games, the nights for drinking and talking and dancing. I preferred the nights, using the time to catch up and reconnect with sisters I only saw once or twice a year, but the games could be just as fun. They were an excuse to be a child again, something that happened so rarely in my day-to-day life that I'd never pass on the opportunity.

First game voted in after breakfast: tag. Fae tag was nothing like the sort of game that human children played. Fairies were fast—like blink and you'll miss them fast. While I knew some of my more hungover sisters, Catriona included, wanted to play so they could hide in the landscape and hunker down for a nap, the more alert among us knew you couldn't let your guard down for even a second.

Because sometimes a second was all it took for someone to tag you—and just like children, no one wanted to be *It*.

As I scanned the environment, on the hunt for the current unfortunate It, I took note of the ample foliage. The maples. The birches. You just didn't get anything like this in the city, not with their beautiful canopies of fresh green leaves, far enough from spring to be lush and beautiful, but still weeks from fall that they held their crisp greenness that we fae were drawn to. If I came up here by myself, I was sure I could lose hours and hours just staring at the trees.

That being said, elves were undeniably worse than fairies when it came to appreciating nature. While I could watch the wind rustle through the leaves and branches, or spend a day in a meadow admiring each flower, an elf could lose themselves for months, unable to resist the siren call of the wild. The outdoors was like crack to an elf; at least fairies maintained their dignity. I could appreciate beauty without getting mind, body, and soul lost in it.

Just as I found myself admiring the black knots in a stark white birch, the only one surrounded by a cluster of maples, a twig snapped underfoot behind me. I whipped around, eyes wide, to see one of my sisters—Adriana—sneaking up on me. We both froze, gazes locked, before I turned and shot off with a half-shriek, half-giggle. She pursued, hot on my heels, our two blurs cutting through the forests and up the mountain slopes, but I eventually managed to lose her after jumping some thickets and skirting across a stream.

Chest heaving, I crouched behind a fat maple, its whole trunk enough to hide me away, a ridiculous smile on my face, and listened to the world settling around me.

"Too slow, Adriana," I muttered.

"Or did I do it to tire you out?" Her voice appeared from somewhere behind me, and I tore off into the wilderness with another laugh. The sun shone brightly, the birds chirped contentedly, and the forest at the base of our mountain retreat seemed to swell with happiness at our presence.

And why shouldn't it? Mother Nature always recognized her sweetest, most mischievous children...

When we let her.

Fun and games were put on hold after lunch when the arrival of a new batch of fae sisters traipsed up the mountainside. There were always a few who had to be fashionably late, but this was kind of ridiculous.

"Oh, of course," Belladonna said, sighing. "Hardly surprised she is the reason they're late."

I sat up on my knees from my place around the fire pit, which we had used to cook our fish lunch paired with an over-abundance of pre-made kale salads. Seriously, could we be any more stereotypical? I'd managed to conjure up a cheeseburger for Catriona earlier for breakfast, but it left me more depleted than I would have liked. So, I sucked it up and shoved big pieces of kale leaves drizzled in some weird, slightly too vinegary dressing into my mouth and pretended it was the best thing since sliced bread. The fish, meanwhile, splurged on from Alfheim by the organizers, had the taste and consistency of salmon, but because it was from a magic-heavy realm, we could order the filets without the iron. Same with the kale in the human world, fish and many dark leafy greens were a rare delicacy that we had to very carefully prepare.

"Who?" I asked, unable to see around my clustering fae sisters, all clamoring and chattering as they swarmed the new arrivals.

Belladonna went back to her food, stabbing her fork at the final bits and pieces of her salad. "Jasmine."

"Oh." Any excitement I might have felt wheezed right out of me, and I sat back down with a roll of my eyes. "I'd hoped she might skip this year."

"She never skips a year," Belladonna bemoaned, "but we should say our hellos. No need to be overtly rude."

I stayed seated while my sister rose. "No, that's her style, I guess."

Lips pursed, I grasped Belladonna's outstretched hand and eased myself up, wiping the dust from my shorts before joining the herd. Things had been going so smoothly, so calmly, and now Jasmine was here to shit all over that.

Don't get me wrong. I loved all my fae sisters—but the degree of my love varied. Catty and bratty Jasmine ranked somewhere near the bottom of my affection scale, and unless she'd had a massive personality overhaul since last year, that wasn't going to change anytime soon.

As always, Jasmine marched at the head of the pack, arms outstretched to block the sisters behind her so that she was in the spotlight. I fell in line behind Belladonna, but I could still see the coils of tight black weaving down around Jasmine's pointed, delicate facial features. She was like a husky, the ones with the piercing blue eyes and dark fur. In many respects, she had the demeanor of a husky too: aloof, distant, uppity. Unless you were so far up her ass, she tasted you, I guess.

My fae sisters flocked in to hug her, embracing her as one of the older, more respected fairies present. She and Belladonna air-kissed, neither groveling as technically they were on the same plane as far as aged respect went. When Jasmine's ice blues fixed on me, I immediately noted all the ways they were different from Catriona's incredibly pale blue eyes. Catriona's were still somehow warm and kind. Jasmine's gaze had that piercing quality that shot straight through you, assessing every flaw with rapid speed and apparent disinterest, like you weren't worth her time.

"Kaye," she greeted, ushering me into her arms like a goddess might her lowliest servant—putting on a show for the people. I offered two stiff back pats with one hand, the other hanging in a loose fist by my side. "Always the black sheep of the herd, sister."

"Good to see you too, Jasmine," I muttered, then rolled my eyes harder than I should as she stroked my hair, my chin resting on her bony shoulder.

"I see you're still working to get a handle on the weight thing. Don't worry. You'll beat it one day," she mused when we broke apart. My eyes flashed a warning I was sure she saw, but she merely smiled and offered a tinkling giggle before moving on to the rest of her adoring subjects.

Fucking... bitch. She's the kind of self-assured narcissist who can break a person down while wearing a breathtaking smile. Yet when I was younger, I was part of the pack who craved her attention. Thankfully, once I was out of high school, I saw straight through her phony charade.

I couldn't say the same for the rest of my sisters, many of them still oohing and ahhing over her floaty sky blue gown, like a millennial hippie straight out of Coachella. Drawing a deep breath, I swallowed my instant annoyance with her, before moving on. After all, there were other sisters to greet, many of whom would be passed over or ignored for the sake of appeasing the resident Queen Bee.

So, I put on a forced smile and pulled the nearest new arrival into a hug. There were too many other sisters here for me to spend time with; Jasmine was not going to ruin this weekend. No matter how many snippy underhanded insults I had to endure, I absolutely refused to let her spoil my good time.

Still, though. What a bitch.

~

My sisters oohed and ahhed over me later that evening, right after I added a splash of near neon green to our Illumination display overhead. Well into the night, a few hours after dinner, Ulia had thrown a blast of purple light over the fire, laughing as the heat carried it up. The wards had eventually snagged it, keeping the light magic from rising out and into view of unsuspecting humans. Ulia's random burst of magic had sparked a light show, with fae sisters seated around our large bonfire contributing with splashes of whatever color they desired.

The outcome was stunning. An array of light and vibrant color. A rainbow that couldn't sit still, and morphed into different shapes and patterns. Whatever lingering tension I felt from Jasmine's arrival faded away as we worked in tandem to create a living, breathing piece of art.

Illumination had always been my favorite type of magic. Even if it wasn't the most useful, it was the first fae-born skill I conquered as a kid. To this day, seeing color glow from the tips of my fingers, or the palms of my hands, brought a blessed sense of ease to my day. If I found myself walking home alone at night from the subway, a gentle pulse of soft off-white in my palms, easily mistaken for a cell phone screen, made me feel safe until I reached my destination.

Although light conjuring wasn't especially useful in a fight, neither a defensive or offensive form of magic, I'd heard stories that it sent vampires and demons and other night-dwelling supers running if you chose the right hue. In a pinch, it would do.

"Someone's craving Christmas," I noted when Catriona added a burst of red threading through my green light, her hair crackling with magic. Even if humans had noticed our show, the simpler of the lot would think they were somehow seeing the Northern Lights... all the way down here in New York.

"I always think they pair so well together," she said dreamily, head cocked back as she watched the lights intermingle, bowing toward one another and then swirling into each other's arms as if engaged in some great, magical dance. It was stunning.

The stunning moment was spoiled, however, when Jasmine stomped through our circle and sent a few of my sisters shuffling so she could have prime real estate in front of the fire. She shivered dramatically, as if that excused her behavior, and tightened her velvety blanket around her before extending her feet toward the bonfire.

"Ugh, what is that smell?" she demanded, nose in the air as she scanned the circle. "Don't you all smell that?" When we murmured answers—all I smelled was bonfire and a bad attitude, but I didn't say that—she huffed and crossed her arms. "Smells like dirty shifter out here." A shiver shot right down my spine. "I've been catching whiffs of it all day."

"There's nothing inside our wards," Belladonna countered from the other side of the fire. Lily and Rose were half-asleep and leaning against her, blinking sleepily at the flames. "Whatever you're smelling must be coming from inside your nostrils."

A few of us giggled and I noted the way Jasmine's cheeks darkened.

"No. I know what I smell." She sniffed noisily once more. "It's a fucking shifter."

In all fairness, I hadn't showered since my run-in with Darius the Dragon in the cave last night. And, considering we ended the meet-up with a little face-eating, I probably had his scent on me. It would have faded over the course of the day, and no one else had said anything. Jasmine must just be hyper-sensitive.

And an attention whore, but that's beside the point.

"I dated one once, you know," she admitted after a few beats had passed. I rolled my eyes and tossed up a pastel purple flash of light, shooting it toward the cluster of other gathered pastels, as Jasmine nodded. Maybe she thought our sisters were staring at her with wide-eyed curiosity, but I couldn't imagine that being the case. "Yes, as humiliating as it is to admit... I did, in fact, slum it with a beast once. I don't know what I was thinking. Such a degrading thing to admit to."

I bit the insides of my cheeks to keep from snapping at her. Catriona must have noticed the way I stiffened, because as other sisters chimed in to comfort Jasmine, Catriona pinched my thigh and shot me a pointed look.

*I'm not going to say anything*, I tried to tell her with my eyes. We both went back to adding color to our floating mosaic, trying to ignore the conversation going on around us.

"I don't think I'll ever be totally clean again," I heard Jasmine whine. "It was like sleeping with an animal. A filthy, disgusting animal. They ought to be banned from Alfheim completely."

"Jasmine." Belladonna's voice issued a warning, one that my least favorite sister was happy to ignore.

"If I could help it, I'd just get rid of them all," she continued. Much to my surprise, a few around the circle nodded along vehemently to every hateful word. "They serve no purpose. Just like humans. I think the worlds would be better off without either of them polluting up our atmospheres."

My hands fell to my lap, and, unable to stop myself, I turned and gawked at her. She caught me staring and shrugged.

"What?" she snapped. "You can't deny it. They don't deserve to live—"

"What a horrible thing to say," I snapped back. "What a *hateful* thing to say. Every creature in this world, and the next deserves to live. Don't be ridiculous, Jasmine."

"Yeah," Catriona said, jumping in before Jasmine or any of her supporters had a chance to contradict me, "you're killing our vibe."

A few of our sisters laughed again, and just like that the conversation switched to something much less polarizing, many resuming our game of creating a gorgeous rainbow overhead.

Later that night, as Catriona and I lay in my messy pile of pillows and blankets, this time sans tarp so we could look at the stars, I glanced over at her, unable to shake Jasmine's words—and Darius's lips—from my mind.

"Do you put any stock in what she had to say tonight?"

"Hmm?"

"Jasmine. Her idea that the world would be better without shifters."

Catriona scoffed, her arms crossed and brow knitted. "Of course not. She's always been a snob about these kinds of things. I didn't think she had any extremist leanings. I didn't think any of our sisters did, but I guess there's always at least one surprise that rattles you at these things."

I bit my lower lip for a moment, plump and fuller than most of the fae I knew, and sighed. "Yeah, I guess."

It was hard to shake the anger from my mind, however, and it mingled with flashes of images and feelings revolving around Darius—who hadn't once come down from his cave to find me. Even as I fell asleep beneath the stars, my head continued to swim, and the dreams that followed were distressed, full of strife and conflict between shifters and supernaturals.

And Jasmine's smug face was there, right in the middle of it all, haunting me until morning.

Sunday rolled around in no time at all, as it always did. In the morning, a few of my sisters were weepy at the start of our last day, but we managed to enjoy ourselves nonetheless.

There were more magical games to be had, meals in front of the fire, and fae-wine for all to savor one last time.

Unfortunately, I found myself struggling to get a certain dragon out of my head. For the better part of the day, Darius had lingered in my mind; the phantom caress of his fingers along my arm, down my neck, sent random chills through my body, tearing me away from whatever activity I should have focused on and bringing me back to him instead.

I hadn't heard or felt him for the rest of the weekend, and yet there was his smiling face—what I remembered of it, anyway. While Jasmine didn't complain about scenting a shifter anymore, she brought up how miserable they were every chance she got, dragging down the group conversation to something awkward and tense where before it had been spritely and free.

As we packed up with the setting sun, Catriona sniffling and whimpering at the thought of being apart—silly thing, we only lived two hours away by train—I decided enough was enough. Clearly, my subconscious had other plans for Darius the Dragon: namely that it wouldn't let me forget him. So, once I had my things stored away in my bottomless bag, I told Catriona I'd be back momentarily— "One last walk into the mountains!"—and flitted toward the path that led to Darius's cave. I passed Jasmine on the way, who, big surprise, had others packing her things for her. She shot me a narrowed look, but I merely rolled my shoulders back and pressed on without a word. She hadn't made me snap yet, besides my brief defense of shifters and humans last night, and she wasn't going to.

My smile faded, however, the more I climbed. Last time the pull had been so intense. My feet knew where to walk because something unseen guided them through the dark. Now, the sun still shone, but I felt clumsy in my finding of the cave. Unfortunately, as soon as I rushed down the tunnel and made it to the inner sanctum did I understand why.

Darius was gone.

I stood stiff and still as I stared at the remnants of his fire.

The soot and ash were cold. He'd been gone at least a day. My hand tightened around my phone, which I'd brought with the intention of swapping numbers.

Fine. Leave then. Not like I care, or anything.

With a huff, I turned and stalked back down to camp, trying not to let his absence bother me, hurt me—but knowing that it already had.

❧ 3 ❧

"WELL, HEY, KAYE THE FAE."

I dropped my keys on the ground, as my heart jumped straight up into my throat, when the last voice I ever expected to hear in the city, sounded behind me. After hastily squatting to grab my mammoth key chain, upon which lived all the keys I needed to keep my business premises safe, I whirled around to make sure I hadn't imagined it. My soft gasp, followed by the quickening of my pulse, told me I had not, in fact, dreamed up Darius's voice out of thin air.

Because there he was, standing right in front of me, grinning in that sexy way that sent a shiver of heat up my spine. Dressed in a black tee—*hellooo* biceps, welcome back into my life—and a pair of clean, crisp dark jeans that fit just right, he looked like every other model wandering around New York City. Only most of those models were too self-absorbed to stop and pester me while I was trying to lock up for the evening.

"Darius," I said curtly before turning back and shoving a key into the front door's lock—only it was the wrong key, so I had to fumble around and try to get the right one into the lock, with trembling fingers and a skyrocketed heartbeat, while his eyes burned holes in the back of my head.

Oh, and did I mention that all I could think about as he was standing behind me, was his soft lips on my skin, and his masculine scent that made me want to rub my body all over his?

"Why the frosty reception, fairy?"

"Why the stalker-serial-killer routine, shifter?" I fired back, then bit the insides of my cheeks to keep from saying anything else. A week had crawled by since I last saw him, and I'd spent most of that time trying to push him out of my head and forget that he had totally bailed right when I opted to let my guard down. No one knew about his rejection but me, of course, but that didn't make it sting any less. The good ol' ego was still bruised, and I wasn't the type to easily forget that.

When I turned to face him again, he was studying me with a slight frown, one that he swapped out for a teasing smirk when I placed a hand on my hip.

"I didn't mean to scare you," he offered, like a naughty, gorgeous schoolboy who'd just been caught misbehaving by the teacher he was about to fuck. I inhaled deeply, refusing to let that shtick work on me.

I didn't want to stand here and do this. I'd had a long day; Karen, my psychiatrist colleague, was out sick so I had to take on all her patients who wouldn't reschedule. We shared many patients—those who were comfortable spilling their guts to two mental health professionals, that is—but I hadn't pulled a full ten-hour day, back-to-back clients, in a while now. And fuck it. I was tired. And Darius had left the mountain range, through the wards somehow, without so much as a good-bye-thanks-for-sucking-face on the way.

So yeah. I wasn't obligated to entertain him on the front stoop of my work—which Karen and I shared with other health professionals, including a massage therapist, an acupuncturist, and an ENT practice. I was the last one out for the day. I had the great honor of locking everything up and dealing with any whiners if a hair was out of place the following morning.

"Okay, well, it's been sweet—"

"No, wait." He blocked my path with that magnificently hulking frame of his, then lifted his hands innocently when I arched an eyebrow. "I'm not here to bother you, I swear. I... I think you're in danger."

I tossed my head from one side to the other with the intent on getting the crick out of my neck, totally unfazed. "What?"

"I had a dream that you were in danger, and I—"

"Yeah?" I smoothed a hand down my knee-length black dress, fitted snug in all the right places with little capped sleeves. "And I had a dream I owned a three-headed dog. Contrary to popular belief, however, Cerberus is not waiting for me at my apartment. So, if you'll excuse me."

My attempt to step around him was once again blocked, and I debated bringing a pedestrian into this as a distraction—or using a pulse of magical energy to shove him back. Neither were ideal, but at least I'd get away from him.

"Kaye, I don't take dreams lightly," he insisted, brow furrowed in a way that was just too damn attractive to ignore. Still, I focused my gaze on a spot over his shoulder instead. "I had the dream the night I left the cave, and I've had it every night since. I can't explain why I know, but Kaye, I honestly believe your life is in serious danger."

"No, you can't know," I said briskly. "You're a shifter, not a super. Premonitions aren't exactly your strong suit."

His jaw clenched for a moment, the muscles flaring on either side of his face like he was biting down hard on his back teeth. Exhaling deeply, I shoved my keys in my purse and cocked a hip. For all my bark and bite, I wasn't a total monster. Either he was genuinely worried about me—which was kind of sweet—or he couldn't think of a better way to follow-up after our make-out marathon in his cave. Whatever the true reasoning behind it, I couldn't help but feel slightly flattered.

Not that I'd let it show, of course.

And not that I actually believed I was in danger. I was a New York City psychologist. I migrated between my apartment, my office, and a martini bar on a regular basis. I had a small circle of local friends but otherwise kept to myself. I didn't engage in Alfheim supernatural politics, so there was no reason for me to be in danger. I was a nobody—just a fairy trying to make her way in the world.

"Okay," I muttered, after a bit of temple rubbing and internal debate. "Okay. So, you think I'm in danger."

"Kaye, personal security, and safety are what I do for a living," Darius countered, eyebrows twitching up slightly. "I *know* you're in danger. I'd like to offer my services to make sure nothing happens."

I bit back a grin as some of my previous anger eased out of me, my stiff shoulders relaxing slightly. "Your services, huh? And what will that entail?"

"I'll make sure your home is safe," he said, as he listed each item off with his fingers. "Check out the safety of your building and office. Sweep the area for magical bugs—"

"I think I would have a better handle on that than you," I interjected, this time holding back a laugh, "but go on."

"Kaye, I know we don't know each other very well, but I don't take this lightly," Darius insisted, and I noted the way his words took on a very faint accent the more passionate he spoke. That made me sigh again.

"How'd you expect me to react to all this?" I gestured between him and me, frowning. "I mean, we met by chance in the mountains *inside* magical wards. We kissed. We parted ways. I went back to see you the night I was supposed to leave—"

"You came back for me?" He seemed genuinely surprised at the notion.

"Yeah, well, you weren't there, so it doesn't matter."

We studied one another for, oh, a few seconds—but it felt like centuries of staring into each other's eyes. His gray orbs had darkened the more impassioned his pleas became, which struck me as odd. Must be a shifter thing. Finally, I looked away, watching the rush of yellow taxis racing by like blurs, trying to beat the post-work gridlock.

"I haven't been able to stop thinking about you," he admitted softly, this time taking me by surprise. "I only left because I had business to attend to, not because I wanted to go." Something pulsed through me at his omission, followed swiftly by a tightness in my chest that made me throw my shoulders back and try to stretch it out. When Darius stepped closer, I inched back, catching my heel on a crack in the sidewalk. His arm shot out to steady me—and didn't let go, as he added, "And it isn't just because I'm dreaming about you every night, Kaye the fae."

My lower lip caught between my teeth as I tried to gauge his sincerity. A guy who looked like Darius obviously had no problem picking up women. Hell, this could just be an act for all I knew, but if so, it was a damn good one. In the end, I decided the darkening of his eyes would be my truth-gauge. We were all adept at hiding our true feelings. Fae were especially skilled at saying one thing while meaning another—but you couldn't fake biology.

"Okay," I said. "I believe you. Sort of. Partially."

We both grinned as his hand fell away, and I found myself missing its firm presence just above the crook of my elbow. Shaking my head slightly, I stepped away from the purple door marked with all our business plaques and quirked an eyebrow.

"I'll let you check out my building and my apartment," I told him, then pointed an accusatory finger at him when his grin slipped into sexy-smirk territory, "but if you *do* follow-through on the whole... stalker-serial-killer routine, I'm throwing you off my balcony, and I live on the sixteenth floor."

He raised his hands again, the twist of his lips doing awful things to my insides. "Fair enough."

When he didn't steer me toward a parked car, I just assumed we were going to walk back to my building. The subway was always madness this time of day, and while my feet demanded I sit down somewhere *immediately*, I could tough out the half-hour walk.

"You know, this is really unprofessional of you," I noted as our leisurely stroll came to a halt at a crosswalk, waiting for the light to change. When he drew a breath, presumably to tell me he didn't stalk and corner *all* his new clients until they accepted his help, I continued with a shrug. "Making me *walk* home when you could just fly me there."

"Not without my wings," he said, not missing a beat. My playful demeanor dropped instantly, head swiveling in his direction sharply, and it looked as though he was having an outbreak of foot-in-mouth disease—only he'd said something embarrassing about *himself*, not me.

"W-What?" As far as I was aware, all dragons had wings. Not that I knew any personally outside of Darius, but the lore always had them soaring overhead, all smug and hoarder-like. "How do you not have wings?"

"Never mind."

"No, tell me," I pressed as we moved in time with the crowd waiting to cross the street. "Do you *literally* not have wings? Because it's no big deal. *I* don't have wings either—"

"I have wings," he said, voice low and terse. He then glanced over both shoulders like someone might be listening, and I wanted to remind him that we were in the city: no one gave two shits about anyone else in New York City. We all just wanted to get where we were going with a minimal amount of hassle.

"So...?"

"So they're..." He gritted his teeth briefly. "They're not working right now."

"Performance issues?" I tried to keep a straight face when he scowled at me. "It's very common. Most men experience it at least once in their lives, and—"

"A witch cursed me, okay?" Noticeable heat rose to his cheeks when he admitted it, and I instantly felt bad for him. I mean, I was born without wings. I'd never known the pleasure of unfurling them somewhere far from prying human eyes and taking to the wind, flying just as naturally as one breathes. I craved wings, of course. I knew many fairies who'd won the genetic lottery and were born with them. I just wasn't so lucky, and it was probably the one thing I would change about myself if I could. I would love, *love* to have wings.

But I didn't know the joys of flying.

Darius had tasted the freedom of soaring and had it taken from him. Poor guy. Guilt seeped through me for the way I'd poked the bear with my teasing.

"Sorry," I managed in the awkward silence that followed.

"Ehh, it's fine," he said with a shrug. We both skirted around a street performer who seemed hell-bent on getting audience participation going. Once we were passed the noise, Darius added, "Just don't piss off someone who can, I don't know, turn you into a toad or brew a potion that smells like beer but will make you puke your guts out."

"Or take away your wings."

"That too."

"And I'm pretty sure that potion was just beer—"

"I'm not a lightweight."

I smirked as we stopped at yet another crosswalk, waiting. "That doesn't surprise me."

As we stood there, I did a quick up and down sweep of the shifter, noting the way he scanned the area, a head taller than me and steely eyes that glinted in the slowly falling early evening sun. Why was he doing this for me? Even if I was in danger, so what? Who was I to him?

I bit the insides of my cheeks when the light changed, walking fast to keep up with his long strides, and when I couldn't hold it in anymore, I blurted, "So what'd you do to make a witch curse you?"

"It's not something I really want to get into," he told me, some of his playfulness from our previous banter faltering. "Seriously."

"Well..." I came to a dead stop, ignoring the people who bumped into me. Pedestrians cursed as I parted the sidewalk like the Red Sea. "I want to know."

"Kaye, *seriously*, we don't know each other well enough to get into that." His jaw clenched again and from the twitch of his hand, it looked like he wanted to grab me and carry on. I held firm, arms crossed.

"That's right, we don't. And finding out what you did to piss off a witch is going to tell me a lot about you in just a few words." I raised a challenging eyebrow when his eyes narrowed. "So either you tell me, or I'm out."

He groaned my name—sexily, if that was possible—and ran a hand through his hair.

"Those are my terms," I stated, grounding myself down hard on the off-chance he might try to drag me onward. Not that he knew where we were going. In theory. I mean, I'd like to think he didn't know the exact location of my building, but he found me at work easily enough.

"Look, we..." Darius beckoned for me to follow him away from the flow of foot traffic, and we stood under the awning of a flower shop, my arms still crossed and hip cocked to one side, waiting. He rolled his eyes as he exhaled deeply. "The witch and I dated for a bit. I wasn't feeling it. I broke things off. She took it really hard."

My eyebrows shot up. "That's it?"

"Yeah."

We stared at one another.

"Darius."

"*Fine.*" Like a little boy, honestly. "I left her for another woman. The witch was a woman scorned. And I finally learned that the old saying has merit. A woman scorned and all that. She took away my wings because I didn't grieve the death of our relationship long enough."

I pursed my lips as I mulled over the information. "Did you cheat?"

"No," he said, just fast enough for it not to be a lie.

"Not even emotionally?"

"We were done and over with. I... I hurt her feelings. It was a shitty thing to do, and now I'm paying for it."

Hmm. I could live with that. Although I still didn't know him well enough yet to gauge a truth from a lie. If I had the chance, I'd do a little more digging later, but for now, he had mollified me.

"Well, okay then." I started walking again, taking it at my own pace this time as I mulled over his story. We were two blocks over and one down when I finally piped up out of my musings. "Why didn't she just look into your true heart?"

Witches were rare supernaturals who had the ability to truly see what was in a person's heart. Most struggled to lie to a fairy, but it was almost downright impossible to lie to a witch.

Darius shrugged again. "Maybe she did. Maybe she just didn't want to believe it. I don't know."

"Well, whatever the reason, I'm sorry you lost your wings." And I meant it. The very idea made my heart heavy in ways I didn't fully understand. "Is there anything you can do to get them back?"

"She set some terms," Darius said stiffly. "I'm... I'm working on them."

While I wanted to press him for more, I knew he had shared more than enough already.

"Work faster, shifter," I teased, hoping the change in tone would lighten the mood, "because I'm sick of walking everywhere."

His lips twitched into a half-smile, which I took as a victory.

"Come on," I tugged him around the corner and onto my street. "My building's this way. Don't judge the carpet in the lobby."

"Ugly lobby carpet? Yeah, I'll be all over that. Not only am I here to ensure your protection, this is also a surprise make-over show. Don't you see all the cameras?"

"Oh, bless my lucky stars!" I cried, fanning myself as he grinned, this time more genuinely. "You're all I've ever wanted in a man!"

He ducked low, his eyes ensnaring mine, and purred, "You have *no* idea, fairy."

In an instant, my cheeks matched my hair, and I hurried toward my building with a scowl as Darius followed along behind me, laughing.

~

"No, no, you keep the change," I insisted, trying to politely close my door on my usual delivery guy. He never wanted to keep the change, no matter how many times I explained to him that it was a tip. Because he was always here in under the estimated time. And my food was consistently hot and delicious. And he did a good job. And *deserved* a hefty tip.

He tried to push at least half back on me, insisting that it was too much, but I shook my head.

"No, that's just enough." I then closed the door in his face, hoping I didn't come across as rude. Ryan had been delivering to me for as long as I'd lived in my current apartment. The doorman knew him by now. He was part of my city family. But I wasn't going to let him short-change himself just because his boss was a dick about tips. Hopefully, he had the good sense to hide away the extras so it wouldn't get taken by someone who hadn't earned it.

Rolling my shoulders back, I cracked my neck with a sharp jerk side-to-side, then locked Darius and I in for—well, maybe just the duration of our takeout dinner, maybe longer.

Although I'd had slight reservations about bringing him up to my apartment, to his credit, the shifter did a full sweep of the area when he arrived. There were no innuendos about falling into bed together, no *give me a tour of the master suite, wink-wink* to be heard. He appeared to genuinely be doing a job, which, I gotta be honest, a part of me hadn't expected.

Mind you, he didn't have any tools with him, so I wasn't exactly sure how he planned to sniff out any magical bugs and whatnot. Another day, he told me. For now, my apartment was clean from things less sinister, like peepholes in my bathroom walls and broken latches over my bedroom window next to the fire escape.

Darius also ducked down to the lobby to ask some questions of my doorman, an errand I did *not* accompany him on. Instead, I dragged my weary body into the shower, and when I returned, the dragon shifter had been flicking through TV channels with his feet up on my coffee table, shoes and all.

*That* did not go over well and ended with him spraying and scrubbing the scuff marks away.

But here we were, three hours later. Normally I'd be talked out after a day of listening and helping clients, but the words just didn't stop. At this point, I couldn't even remember exactly what we talked about; the conversation flowed seamlessly from one topic to another, until finally, our rumbling tummies were too much to ignore.

Take out bags in hand, I found Darius in my galley kitchen pouring two glasses of water.

"I couldn't find anything else fun to drink," he noted as I set our dinner down on the counter, the space rather tight with the two of us puttering around. "I also assumed you weren't in the mood for a glass of straight vodka."

I smirked, eyes darting up to my alcohol shelf on top of the fridge. Primarily spirits, a few of the bottles had been replaced with the good stuff from Alfheim, but since I had the occasional human visitor, I didn't want anyone asking about the strange labels written in old fairy languages.

"No, I don't think so." I eased around him to the fridge, my cheeks prickling with heat when our bodies brushed together. "I swear I had a few beers in here, though."

"None for me. I want to stay sharp for the night watch."

I closed my fridge harder than necessary. "Excuse me?"

"I figured I'd stay the night," he told me—like it was no big deal. "Just until I can properly fortify the place." He must have noticed my expression, a smooth blend of shock, outrage, and mild arousal. "I'll sleep on the couch, of course. I won't do much sleeping, so you don't need to worry about me."

"Huh." I leaned against the fridge, then hastily scrambled to catch the magnets I'd knocked off. Once I had them back in place, I swept my hair behind my ears, noting the way his eyes fixated on the motion of my hand. "Well, glad I extended the invite."

"Me too." He shot me a wink before turning on the sink and filling the second glass to the brim. "Water good?"

I snorted. "Uh. Not really."

He turned the sink off and faced me, our bodies mere inches apart, despite us both leaning on opposite sides of the kitchen. "Why?"

"Because..." I motioned to the glass, surprised he didn't just *know*. "There's iron in tap water." He looked down at it, frowning. "And... iron is like fairy kryptonite?"

"I knew that," Darius muttered, dumping what I guessed was going to be my glass back into the sink. "I didn't know you were all *that* sensitive."

"It's a gift," I said with a sigh, rolling my eyes. I then busied myself getting plates and cutlery, stomach at peak howling point now. "Some fae use charms and trinkets on their taps, like a water filter, and it does a pretty good job of getting rid of any excess minerals. Others try to spell it away. I, on the other hand," I went back to the fridge and retrieved a bottle from the back, "buy in bulk from Alfheim because I know it's pure."

His face twisted into something unreadable for a moment, which I chose to ignore, before mumbling, "Makes sense, I guess."

After we both loaded our plates with takeout, Darius

hoarding all the dumplings for himself, we migrated back to the living room. Whatever weird reaction he'd had to my mention of Alfheim had passed, as evidenced by the somewhat cheeky smile he shot me.

"So what about showers? What do you do for that?"

"I shower, if that's what you're asking."

"You *do* smell pretty awesome. It's a quandary."

"I tap into my white magic supply when I shower," I stated, biting back the urge to tell him he smelled pretty delicious too—for a shifter. Because that would be rude. And telling. "I can usually last about ten minutes, maybe less, so I have to power-wash most days."

"Only ten minutes?" Darius arched an eyebrow. "So, no time for shower sex, huh?"

I fought against the blush washing over my cheeks and instead, reached for the remote nonchalantly to turn on the TV.

"Or," I said, then looked him dead in the eye, "*only* enough time for shower sex."

He choked on a dumpling.

"YOU KNOW, IF YOU REALLY WANT TO INVESTIGATE A PLACE that's detrimental to my health, Ballard's Ice Cream bar is probably the place to start." I scooped a spoonful of strawberry cheesecake ice cream into my mouth, savoring the addition of raspberries and chocolate chips I'd added liberally down at the shop.

"You know..." Darius licked his spoon, remnants of his chocolate-cookie-monster deluxe carried away by his tongue. He lifted a foot to my balcony railing and tipped his chair onto its two back legs, smirking. "Pretty sure I'm not here to fight your calorie demons, but I'll keep that in mind."

I swallowed the urge to tell him that the only thing I was truly in serious danger of, was over-indulging on ice cream.

Instead, I simply spooned another mouthful of deliciousness into my mouth. Today was apparently a junk food day. First Chinese takeout, then ice cream from the make-it-yourself bar at the end of my block. This wasn't my first rodeo down there. The cashiers practically knew my name—and that I always got a large scoop.

But Darius had put up a fuss about the bottle of wine I'd opened, and since he was so intent on staying sober and *not* distracting himself by kissing me, I had needed something to satiate my sweet tooth. So, ice cream it was. He had complained at first, not wanting to leave my apartment tonight because of his weird shifter spidey-senses, but he couldn't deny he'd morphed into a kid in a candy shop the second we were in the store.

My hips were not going to thank me in the morning, but after the insane day I'd had running the practice by myself *and* dealing with a dragon shifter telling me I was in serious danger, I thought I deserved to treat myself.

We ended up on my balcony when we returned. While I enjoyed the fresh, cooler-than-street-level night air, I knew we were out here because we were getting too cozy on the couch earlier, and Darius wanted to be stone-cold sober; apparently, alcohol wasn't the only thing that could get him intoxicated. I was officially on that list now, too.

Awesome. A fucking straight-edge shifter bent on playing my personal protector. Gorgeous *and* untouchable.

At the thought, I shoved an extra-large spoonful of ice cream into my mouth, chewing the cheesecake crust bits with a pout.

"So," Darius started, tipping dangerously far back in his chair. My balcony was usually a comfortable fit for one person; two was pushing it a bit. Heights always reminded me of my inability to fly, so I tended not to use it. We'd had to dust both chairs off before they were suitable for sitting.

"So?"

"You were telling me about your family?"

I stabbed at a frozen strawberry. "Was I?"

"Can you?"

"Why?"

Darius shrugged. "Why not?"

Because families were touchy subjects for a *lot* of people, supernaturals, and humans alike. For all he knew, my home life could have been one big epic disaster, and talking about it would trigger a Greek-goddess worthy meltdown.

Fortunately, that wasn't the case. Sort of. I'd grown past my childhood misfortunes.

"I don't know. I have one?" I ate another spoonful of ice cream, thoughtful as I noted him watching me out of the corner of my eye. "Well. I *used* to. My mom died during childbirth with me. Dad couldn't handle looking at me, so he dumped me and my brother with my aunt and left."

"Shit. Sorry, Kaye, you don't have to—"

"It's fine." I stabbed at the next piece of frozen fruit with more vigor. "My aunt was awesome. So was my brother, until he left." That one hurt more than my dad. "He left when he turned eighteen and didn't look back."

At the time, I'd been devastated—like don't get out of bed for days devastated, sobbing at the drop of a hat devastated. Zayne was my best friend, my protector, my partner-in-crime. We were two parentless brats thrust upon our aunt. It was supposed to bond us for life.

I guess he just didn't feel the same way.

"He sounds like an ass," Darius said as he came back onto all fours of his chair. I also noted I was working through my ice cream *much* faster and should probably slow down. "I've got a couple of asshole brothers too, but I love 'em."

"You kind of have to." Even though he too had abandoned me, I still loved Zayne. Deep down, under the anger and wounded feeling of intense betrayal. He was my big brother. I'd always love him.

When Darius went quiet, I prodded him with my foot. "What about you? Spill it, dragon. It's only fair."

He chuckled. "Not much to share. I'm the oldest of three boys. We were born into the Sanctius dragon shifter clan. My father is a highly respected member. My mother babies all of us, especially my youngest brother. I... I left after the curse."

"Why?" I shook my head. "Couldn't they help you? It wasn't your fault you were cursed. Not really."

Even if he *had* broken the witch's heart, stealing his wings wasn't an appropriate response.

"I want them to respect me," he told me, expression hardening for a moment. "It's... humiliating. A dragon who can't fly. I would never live it down. I had to leave so I could figure out a cure on my own."

"Stubborn." Alpha-personality. Can't let anyone see his weakness. I made note of that if I needed something to explain his stupidity in the future.

"Mom used to say that was my middle name," Darius said, smirking. His face lit up when he mentioned her. I wish I could say the same about *my* mom, but I never knew her and every time I thought about the situation involving her death, I felt somewhat guilty. After all, she died while having me. And despite the fact fairies could heal, no magic was powerful enough to save her from that.

The chair groaned as he twisted his body to face me. "I know this is kind of personal, but are there any shifters in your family?"

I frowned. "Shifters? No, not that I'm aware."

"Huh." He faced away and went back to his ice cream.

"Why?"

"Curious, I guess. You're not like other fairies, that's all."

We sat in silence for a little while, both of us mulling over what we'd learned.

"So," I blurted, mirroring his previous start to a very personal conversation, "tell me how you met the witch."

Darius groaned. "Really?"

"*Do* it."

"We met where everyone meets."

"Bookstore? Gym? Online?"

"A bar."

I laughed. "You're a walking cliché, Darius."

"And what about you?" he fired back. "All this prying into my love life... What about your seedy romantic history?"

"Hardly seedy." I bit my lip, not interested in sharing the family history *and* my pathetic romantic past on the same night, but Darius had been more than open with me. "He was another fairy. It was a year ago. I thought he was the one."

"And?"

"He cheated." My cheeks grew hot as I stuffed two spoonfuls of ice cream into my mouth. Beside me, Darius's expression had hardened again, so I shrugged, not wanting to make a big deal out of it. "I should have guessed that'd be the outcome. Fae men are known to stray. They're too pretty and too interested in shiny things not to wander. It was my fault."

"No, it wasn't." The gruffness of his voice surprised me, and I turned to find him scowling at my railing. "No one deserves to be treated like that. It wasn't your fault, Kaye."

"Well, whoever's fault it was, I stopped dating shortly after." Ice cream complete, I stashed the cup under my seat. "And that's the way I like it."

"I think you should reconsider your feelings about that," Darius insisted. He shot me a sexy grin before turning his gaze out to the city before us, to the sea of lights that made the metropolis of New York, a very beautiful sight.

I studied him briefly, arms wrapped tight around myself. "Maybe I will."

His grin widened, eyes twinkling with our city stars. "I'll hold you to it..."

Good *grief,* am I ever in trouble.

+§+   4   +§+

I AWOKE the following morning alone—and not for lack of trying. Exhaling sleepily, I rolled over to check my clock, which told me that it was about five minutes before my alarm was set to go off. With a few heavy blinks, I turned the alarm off and rubbed at my eyes, wondering if last night with Darius was just a dream.

But, moments later, the rustling of dishes coming from my kitchen told me no, it wasn't. He was still here. He had stayed the night, just like he told me he would. I pinched myself, just to be sure, then sat up and listened to him putter around for a little while. As I tried to run my hands through my mane, I caught the distinctive whiff of bacon. Apparently, he had helped himself to my fridge again, but he was too "professional" to help himself to *me* last night.

I couldn't help it. After our lengthy talks about relationships and family dynamics on my balcony, I had offered him a spot in my bed, all the while knowing he would shoot me down. I guess I was feeling masochistic, because he *did* shoot me down, politely, and insisted he would stand watch this first night instead. Fine. I wasn't someone to beg. But when I leaned up to press a kiss to his cheek, he had turned his face at the last moment and captured my lips with his in a sweet, chaste kiss. Romantic, almost, given the mood lighting from Manhattan's buildings twinkling back at us.

Clearly, I wasn't pulling this sexual tension out of thin air. Darius wanted it. He just wanted to do his job more.

I rolled my eyes and flung my covers back, recalling my jaunt to the bathroom at three this morning. Half-asleep, I'd shuffled out and caught him sitting on my balcony still—this time on the railing itself, watching. On guard. Like a gargoyle overlooking its monastery, only not an asshole. Gargoyles were assholes, from what I'd heard.

The sight had touched me in ways I wasn't ready to properly process yet, so after shimmying into some pajama shorts and throwing a house coat over the whole mismatched ensemble, I headed for my kitchen repressing any, and all, feelings I might have developed since I let a sexy dragon shifter into my apartment.

"Morning," he greeted, a little too chipper for my taste. My *not-a-morning-person expression* made him chuckle, and my features softened when he handed over a mug of steaming hot coffee. "I've tried to make everything without iron, just for my favorite fairy."

"Thanks," I muttered, then took a sip. *Oh.* He meant he didn't use water. That's a *lot* of creamer—but there was a mouth-watering man making me breakfast, so I couldn't complain. The only thing that would have made this better was if he was shirtless, which I'd always assumed was some rule of the Man Code to be half-naked when making bacon. Apparently, Darius hadn't gotten the memo. My eyes swept over him appreciatively before I went to lean against the sink, watching him work with a tilt of my head.

"How did you sleep?" he asked, back to me as he flipped all six—*six!*—pieces of bacon at once.

"Well. You?"

"Didn't sleep."

I slurped my coffee. "Awfully chipper for someone who didn't sleep."

"Comes with the job. All-nighters aren't new to me."

I resisted the urge to ask if shifters were able to withstand sleep deprivation better than most. Even though it was normal to ask about powers and abilities, shifters were touchy about it—probably because we supernaturals made them feel like the lesser species simply because they could only turn into animals. I'd no idea what else a whole magical population in my community was capable of, and, honestly, that didn't sit right with me.

Instead of probing, however, I changed the subject entirely.

"As you can see, I survived the night *without* an assassination attempt." My expression turned smug when he glowered over his shoulder at me. "Looks like, just as I thought, your dreams were merely your subconscious encouraging you to see me again. Case closed."

Darius gave a humorless chuckle as he poked at the sizzling strips of pork. "Hardly."

"What'd 'you mean *hardly?*" I motioned to myself, drawing my hand up and down like I was a game show presenter showing off a really good prize. "I'm alive, aren't I? Pretty sure that makes me right, and you wrong."

"Not necessarily," he told me. I watched him look through all my cupboards for a little while until finally taking mercy and grabbing a plate from the drying rack. He accepted it with a little half-smile, clearly not pleased with my attitude about all this. "Just because you didn't *die* last night doesn't mean you aren't still in danger. That's a black-and-white way of looking at it, Kaye."

I drew in a deep breath, then exhaled it slowly, watching him work and biting my tongue. Sure, my somewhat joking perspective on all this might be black-and-white, but you know what—it was warranted. Never in my life had I ever been in *danger*, and Darius's assertions that suddenly I was, and suddenly I *needed* his protection, wasn't exactly sitting well with me. He hadn't done much to drive the point home, honestly, and I didn't feel any less safe in my cozy old one-bedroom now than I did any other morning.

"Look," I started after he grabbed a carton of eggs from my fridge and cracked two into a pan, cooking them in the bacon grease, "I appreciate your concern. Last night was a lot of fun. I'd like to do it again sometime. But I don't think there's anything to worry about. I'm fine. You're fine. We're all *fine*."

"Kaye—"

"I just don't want you going out of your way to do this just because you dreamt up some ludicrous story that feels too real not to be true, or whatever," I insisted, pinching the bridge of my nose as I pointedly reminded myself *not* to get too analytical on him. I spent most days listening to problems and trying to talk through them. That was what I specialized in: talk therapy. Karen handled the medical side of things at our little practice. Sometimes I slipped and psychoanalyzed issues with my friends, and apparently, that wasn't a very appealing trait.

"I didn't pull this out of thin air," he told me, flipping the eggs, mouth set in a tight line. "I have good instincts. My job has always been to protect people. I *know* when they need protection."

"Maybe." I fiddled with the tie of my housecoat. "And maybe not. All I'm saying is... You can go on with your life. You don't have to spend every night on my balcony on the lookout for phantom dangers—"

"Let's just drop it," he said gruffly. With those eggs done, browned and crispy by the high heat and bacon grease, he dumped them on the plate and added two more to the pan. "I'm not backing off on this."

"Even if I insist?"

"Even if you insist."

*That's what* you *think, dragon.* I rolled my eyes and went back to nursing my coffee. It was *way* too early to have a full-out brawl with the hot shifter cooking me breakfast. So, I let it go for the time being, prepping my very tiny table at the end of the galley, able to see into both the living room and the kitchen. Mostly I used it for mail and bread and odds and ends I couldn't find a place for. This morning, however, I didn't think it appropriate for us to eat such a nice breakfast on the couch in front of the TV like a couple of millennial savages. So, I cleared off all the junk and gave it a quick wipe-down, slightly embarrassed about how much dust had collected there during its disuse.

We ate breakfast in an amicable silence, me checking work emails on my phone and Darius occasionally asking questions about the building—which I did *not* know the answers to. Just because I'd lived here for almost six years didn't mean I actually knew anything about the overall building. There was a laundry room on the first floor and a really shitty gym on the second. Half my utilities were included and I'd never had a plumbing issue. I'd been incredibly fortunate to never have loud neighbors, but every year there was always the risk of that changing.

After, I fought him on doing the dishes, but he insisted that he wanted to be useful. Only a crazy person—so unprofessional of me, I know—fought for longer than necessary to hand wash breakfast dishes, so I left him to take a quick shower and get ready for the day. When I emerged from my bedroom twenty minutes later in a black pantsuit that I always thought made my (rather flat) ass look stellar, he was waiting in the living room with the TV on. Lips pursed, I twisted my wet hair into a knot on top of my head, going for some half-assed ballerina bun thing, and then grabbed the remote.

"Hey," he protested when I turned it off.

"I have to go to work," I said, hoping he would just get the hint. When he stared up at me, I crossed my arms, not once breaking eye contact. "And you're not staying here while I'm out."

*Was this all some elaborate scheme to find a place to live?* Darius didn't strike me as homeless, but there were all sorts in the city, and I wasn't one to judge. Still, he looked and smelled clean, so I hoped I was way off base with that theory.

"I wasn't just going to lounge on your couch and watch TV," Darius argued, sitting up a little straighter. "I had planned to ask for a key so I could run home, get my things, and come back while you were out to set up my protection devices—"

"Like *hell* I would let you dig around my apartment while I'm not here!" I sputtered. I mean, he was gorgeous as sin and charming to no end, but that didn't mean I was ready for him to snoop through my unmentionables while I was at work. "No way, Darius. You gotta be kidding."

"Kaye, I know you think everything is fine, and you're not in danger," he said, either oblivious to my bristling annoyance or just not caring, "but I've been in this business a long time. Shit always hits the fan when you least expect it. I've seen it happen many times before. I've seen clients refuse my help and then things go south while I'm gone."

"So you've had dreams about other people and then spent the night—"

"I've had *consultations*," he stressed, this time sounding more frustrated with me as he stood. The distance between us made the height difference a little more manageable, but I had no problem glaring up at him if I had to. He crossed his arms, biceps bulging just enough to catch my attention.

*No, Kaye. Focus, for fuck's sake, and rein in your damn libido.*

He took a step toward me, but I held firm, wondering if he wanted me to shy away. Fucking alpha men. Always had to be the biggest cock in the roost.

"And were you this insistent about it before?" I demanded. "You always push yourself on people this way, like a maniac?" A look of indignation flashed across his face, which made me sigh. "Look, I've been really open and accepting of all this, but I'm kind of reaching my limit. You're a nice guy, Darius, from what I can tell, anyway, considering I don't know you that well. Yeah, you've been open, honest, and kind to me from the day we met, but that doesn't mean you can just barge into my life and expect me to pry open every nook and cranny in return for you to ogle. It doesn't work like that."

"I'm not asking to know your deepest, darkest secrets," he said after a few beats of tension had passed. His voice softened, and suddenly I just felt tired and my suit felt tight and I wanted to crawl back into bed. Instead, I went for my shoes, and my ears twitched at the soft footfalls padding after me. "I just want to keep you safe, Kaye. Something *feels* wrong, and I know that isn't enough for humans, but *you* should understand that we get feelings like this. We notice shifts in the air. We feel the presence of another shifter or supernatural. I just... That's what's happening around you. I feel it, and I'd never forgive myself if something were to happen because I let you bully me out of here."

I looked up sharply, unable to hide my smile. "I'm not bullying you. I'm being very mature and logical."

"Calling me a maniac isn't bullying? You're a terrible psychologist."

"Fuck you."

We both grinned at one another as the tension eased away. I was still exhausted—the conversation was so draining and I had six more draining chats to have today with clients. How was I going to get through it? No idea.

"Okay, *that* was unprofessional," I said as we faced off, "but I'm not required to be professional in the privacy of my own home."

"I, on the other hand, have been totally professional with you," Darius said, his voice taking on a rumbly growly quality that made my knees weak. "And I'm still here. Fighting with you. Because I believe in what I'm saying. I know you don't know me well enough to trust me, but I'm asking you to go out on a limb here."

"You're not staying inside of my apartment *or* getting my key while I'm at work," I said frankly. "Let's get that straight. Nor," I raised a hand to silence him when he drew a breath, lips quirked into a smile, "are you coming to work with me, following me to work, or doing anything remotely stalkerish. You're just not, Darius. I want to trust you, but you need to give me something to work with."

"How about this?" he said slowly as if mulling over what he had to say in his head for a few seconds first. "I'll make you a deal."

I perked up a little at the mention of a deal, then instantly hated myself. Deals were huge in fae culture. I just couldn't help it. And Darius seemed to notice how he had caught my attention, which only made his smile bloom, much to my embarrassment.

"Ah, that's what I thought." He chuckled. "You fairies. Deals are like catnip to you."

"What is it?" I demanded before pointedly checking my watch. "I need to go open the practice soon."

"I'll leave you alone for today and tonight," Darius stated. "I won't follow you to work or stake out the building across the street from your office. I won't loiter in front of this building like a creep. I won't harass you once an hour to tell me that you're safe."

I rolled my eyes. "Wow, really selling your services there. This all makes me so thrilled about wanting to work with you."

"*If* I successfully back off," he pressed on, fixing me with a slight glare, "then you will agree to take my help—until the job is done. I will be your personal protector until I can be sure the danger is gone and you're in the clear. What do you think?"

Biting my lip, I went for my purse and pretended to check through things, then did the same with my work bag. To me, this phantom danger wasn't a thing—it just wasn't. Clearly, it mattered to Darius or he wouldn't be this adamant about it. If it was all a lie and this was just an excuse to see me, kind of intimately and creepily, then he had some serious mental health issues and I would probably have to hire my own personal bodyguard just to keep him at bay. But from all I had learned about him in the last, oh, fifteen hours, I suspected that wasn't the case.

That wasn't to say there wasn't still *something* there. He could have elements of paranoia and obsession in his personality, but I wasn't in the space to decide whether they were a detriment to himself or others. For now, those habits were just annoying.

"Fine," I said once I had my keys in hand and was practically out the door. "*Fine.* I'll take that deal. You have to be out of sight, *gone*, until tomorrow morning. No calls. No texts. No watching me from the street corner and following me. You have to fuck off completely, *then* I'll take your help until the danger—" I put air-quotes around the word to show him how seriously I took the issue. "—is gone."

"Deal." Darius held out his hand to me. "Shake on it."

That made me hesitate. Deals were sacred. Fairies didn't enter deals lightly.

But the danger wasn't *real*. It couldn't be. He was blowing smoke, and after a night on my own, he would realize just how crazy this all was, and get this protection thing out of his mind.

At least if I made the deal, I was guaranteed to see him again. Outside of all of this your-life-is-in-danger-let-me-be-your-super-hero crap, I actually kind of liked the guy.

So, ignoring the niggling voices at the back of my mind telling me to stop and reconsider, I slid my hand into his and squeezed.

"Deal."

A bolt of electricity shot through both of us, like a static zap after shuffling your feet across the carpet. His eyes widened and I hastily pulled my hand away, rubbing the still tingling palm.

I'd never made a deal before. Not a *real* one, anyway. Apparently, my magic knew the difference.

"Well. That's over with." I pointed to the door, trying to ignore the way my body hummed. I was seeing the world more vividly than before, but like blinking away the swirling colors on your retinas after a flash of blinding light, it faded away within moments, bringing the world back to its regular, dull ordinariness.

*The after-effects of making a deal.* Totally unexpected—and I wasn't comfortable with Darius watching me process these feelings. "You're fun to look at, shifter, but I'm going to be seriously late for work if you don't get the fuck out of my apartment..."

❀  5  ❀

DARIUS KEPT HIS WORD. Not once did I see, hear, or catch a whiff of him for the entire day. Not while I was at work. Not on the subway home. And not around my apartment building. He had upheld the stipulations of the deal—which meant the deal was on. I had awoken to a text from him this morning, well within the rules, in which he told me he would be by after work today to start setting up legitimate protection crap around my apartment. I wasn't thrilled at the idea, but a deal's a deal, and he had every right to help in whatever way he thought necessary.

Still, I wasn't looking forward to finding out exactly what he planned to install in my home. In such a chaotic city like New York, where there were days when just existing drained me to a pulp of mush, I wanted my home to be my sanctuary – my peaceful place where I could just relax and not worry about having to be *on* for people. Sure, it was just a one-bedroom apartment, but it was *my* one-bedroom apartment, and I loved it. I had always felt safe there. It wrapped itself around me like a big, cozy cocoon during terrible storms and after awful, heart-wrenching days at work.

I guess, most of all, I just didn't want Darius to ruin that sanctuary with whatever he had in mind to fight off the "danger" that he seemed to believe was on its way to my doorstep. I'll be honest; I spent most of my day worrying about it—then feeling insanely guilty for not giving my clients as much of my focus and energy as they deserved. Tomorrow, I would be better. Once I knew how this dragon was going to alter my home life, I might actually be able to concentrate again. Until then, I was a twitchy, irritable wreck, despite my deeply buried excitement over the thought of seeing him again.

I arrived home shortly after 5 pm, which was standard on a day where I wasn't swamped with clients and Karen wasn't out sick. My weary bones, worn out mostly from worry, were heavy as I dragged them through the lobby and into the elevator. I only had *maybe* forty minutes before Darius planned to waltz back into my life, which was just enough time to shower, put on something comfortable—my skirt waistline was just *digging* into my stomach—and take a few minutes for myself to breathe.

As the elevator doors swished open, I shuffled out into my hallway—and came to a sudden stop when I spotted something in front of my door. A large box. Head cocked to the side, I reached out into the ether with my magic, testing the area for darkness. With a blink, my vision turned near x-ray, fueled by my innate magical ability, allowing me to see anything beyond the mundane floating around my hallway. When nothing presented itself, I blinked the power away and proceeded toward the box with caution.

I half-expected to see Darius's writing scribbled all over it, but much to my surprise, it was blank. No writing anywhere, not even my address. Frowning, I crouched down and touched the cardboard hesitantly. It felt like... regular cardboard. I glanced down the hall in either direction, feeling a little silly. Paranoid, even. Apparently, Darius had infected me, but with all his talk of danger and now the sudden appearance of a strange box in front of my door... Coincidence? I couldn't be sure.

Teeth gritted, I tapped into my magic again, eyes closed but able to see more than any human ever could. Now that I was closer, I noted a faint pulsing yellow light around the box, which must have blended with the cardboard at a distance. I probed it carefully but found it unyielding and taut. Magic. Someone had placed an enchantment around the box. My frown deepened. It wasn't typical fae magic either; something more potent. When I opened my eyes, I found them watery and my nose runny, the effort it took to poke the magical shield a bigger drain on my abilities than I cared to admit.

At the sound of a door opening down the hall, I scooped the package up, grunting a little under its weight, and brought it inside. No need for my human neighbors to see me crouched over a box, hands up like I was feeling for auras, or whatever.

Once I was inside, however, I couldn't shake the feeling that I did *not* want this thing in my home just yet. With a steadily tightening knot churning in my gut, I headed straight for the balcony and placed the box outside. Then, for good measure, I locked the sliding glass doors and stepped back with a firm nod. There. Try to get at me through *those* babies, box!

My arms slumped to my side. *Right. This was stupid.* The box might not even be for *me*; it wouldn't be the first time a mailman got the wrong unit and didn't care. But that would require there to be an address written somewhere. As far as I could see, there was nothing, not even a tiny bit of scrawl to fuel the magic encasing the package.

So, after changing out of my work clothes and into a pair of black yoga pants and a slouchy dark gray T-shirt, I settled on the armrest of my couch, still in view of the box, and searched around on my phone until I found Clara's number.

Clara, an old friend, was one of the city's most respected mages. Unlike witches, mages dealt primarily in elemental magic. In a way, I always thought they were more hardcore than other supernaturals, using their bodies to channel their craft in ways that could destroy them. Witches played with the fabric of the universe. They used their gifts to control what was already present, creating spells to weave the magic for their use. Mages were conduits. Their bodies were their wands, and water, fire, air, wind, and spirit crafted their power.

At least, that was how I understood the difference. There were so many supers in this world, and the next, that it was hard to keep everybody straight sometimes. All I knew was that Clara Brighton had a lot of tattoos, baked killer cupcakes, and lived in a house crawling with ivy, the sheer number of potted plants inside stifling. Clearly an earth mage. Still, she was one of the few people nearby who I could consult on this, so I clicked around until I found her number, then hit the call button.

As the phone rang, however, I realized how absurd this all was. I could figure this out on my own. A box was just a box until it wasn't, and Clara had a busy life.

So, as soon as she answered, I did the small talk thing and invited her out to lunch, insisting we hadn't seen each other in *too* long. She agreed. Now we had a lunch date for next Saturday, and the knot in my stomach wasn't any smaller.

Nibbling my lower lip, I wandered back to the sliding door in front of my balcony to study the mystery box with a frown. What if it was a gift from someone I knew—maybe Catriona?— and they cloaked it in magic to keep me from spoiling the surprise? No. If that was the case, they would have written something on it to clue me in. This was something...else.

I jumped, and let out a pretty embarrassing gasp when my phone started shrieking and vibrating in my sweaty hand. Heart pounding, I checked the screen; it was the number for the building's intercom system. Darius must be waiting for me to let him in.

"Hello?" I said, somewhat breathlessly as I turned away from the balcony and sauntered slowly across my small living room.

"What's wrong?" Yup, suspicions confirmed: Darius had arrived.

"Nothing. Are you here?"

"Yeah, let me in."

I pressed the number 9 key on my phone, alerting the system

to open the door to the lobby. Just as I was about to hang up, the glass doors behind me shattered. This time there was nothing embarrassing about my scream. I whirled around, eyes wide in a panic, as a grotesque stone gargoyle clambered through what was left of my balcony door, its eyes a sickly yellow, like the magic shield I'd seen around the box, and fixed on me.

My first response was to hurl a flash of bright white light at it, hoping that the appearance of sunshine might send it scrambling—but then I remembered it wasn't a troll and sunshine had no impact on gargoyles. *Fuck.* It surged toward me, its great stone wings carrying it across my living room, and I dove out of the way with another strangled cry, scrambling into my kitchen and searching for a weapon.

And then realizing, in my panicked state, that I *was* a weapon.

Give me a break. It's hard to think straight in a life or death situation!

The gargoyle followed, faster than I would have liked, slamming into my wall and leaving a mammoth dent right down to the concrete. I hurled whatever dishware I could find on the counter and in the drying rack, but that only seemed to make the big hunk of rock angrier. Its roar rattled the whole unit—probably the whole *building*. While I managed to skirt out of the way when it made another lunge for me, I knew it would start cataloging my movements and anticipating my defense.

On their own, gargoyles were dumb as bricks. Gargoyles, however, were animated by magic-users—and they tended to take on their temporary master's personality. Whoever was enough of an asshole to sic a gargoyle on you was bound to have a pretty shitty personality, honestly.

Someone must have shrunk him down, set him on a timer, and placed him in that fucking box.

What the hell had I done to make someone want to send a gargoyle after me?!

"Open the door, Kaye!" The gargoyle stood between me and

the front door, behind which I could hear Darius pounding on. Not wanting to lose yet another doorway—I was never getting my security deposit back now—I waited until the gargoyle lunged, then dropped and rolled beneath him with enhanced fae speed. Back on my feet, I raced for the door, unlocked it with shaky fingers, and got the hell out of the way as Darius came barreling through.

Without a word, he went straight for the gargoyle. As I shoved my front door closed and essentially cowered in front of it, Darius slammed a fist into the animated statue's grotesque square jaw, knocking a chunk of rock off, then managed to get the creature into a headlock. While its wings flapped hard, the force knocking paintings off my wall and glass knick-knacks off my bookshelf, Darius held tight, face red and teeth gritted.

And his eyes... His eyes were like storm clouds.

He gave a guttural snarl as he ripped the gargoyle's head from its shoulders, and within seconds, the body crumbled to the ground, settling at my dragon's feet as dust. The head's eyes continued to burn bright yellow for a few seconds more before slowly losing their color, turning back to slate gray before the head disintegrated in Darius's hands.

"What...?" He looked between my shards of sliding glass door to the upturned furniture, cracked TV screen—*thanks, gargoyle*—and general disarray that my living room and kitchen was in. Then, he turned his glare to me, which I thought was totally unnecessary. *I* was the victim here. Still, that didn't stop him from growling, "What. the hell. happened?"

"I don't know," I snapped back, in no mood for whatever lecture he had on the tip of his tongue—or to hear an I-told-you-so. "I came home and there was a box encased in magic in front of my door. I brought it onto my balcony, and I think...I think the gargoyle was inside."

"Kaye! You should have waited for me—"

"You were on-route," I shouted, voice strangled as I stood and wiped at the warmth trickling down my cheek. *Blood.* When had that happened? "I figured I'd just wait for you to get here and we could tackle it together."

He ran a hand through his deliciously rumpled hair, scowling. "Fuck."

"Yeah, sounds about right."

A wave of pure exhaustion washed over me. Sighing, I rubbed at my face, then puttered into my battered and broken living room, cautiously righting upturned furniture and skirting around the pile of rubble in the middle of it all. If ever there was a time that I wished to know an Angel, it would have been then. Angels could sweep the room with just a hand, and within seconds, everything would be as it once was. But I didn't know any Angels, so I was left standing in a pile of dust and rubble, that was once my apartment.

Darius, meanwhile, just stood there, hands on his hips—fuming. He looked from my shattered balcony doors—the superintendent of my building was going to *kill* me—to the settling chaos all around him.

"Tell me everything," he said, voice all hot and growly again. Shaking, like he was trying to keep it even. I hated that I found him attractive after everything that had just happened.

"Well, I woke up this morning to a text from you—"

"Skip to the good stuff," he ordered sharply, which made me look up in surprise. He was *really* worked up about this. *I* should probably be more worked up about this. Maybe I just wasn't processing it yet. Maybe my brain had thrown up a mask of indifferent numbness to shield me from the fact that someone had animated, and sent me a gargoyle with the express purpose of snapping me like a twig.

My knees gave way suddenly and I collapsed onto the corner of the TV stand, reaching back to steady my cracked TV before I did more damage to it. Darius seemed to want to reach out for me, but he had taken to pacing instead. I understood the feeling.

"I came home and there was this box in front of my door." I glanced out to the balcony, noting that the box had disappeared.

*Perfect.* Did the box turn into the gargoyle? "I tried to use my magic to see what was inside because it didn't have any writing or signage on it, but there was like... a yellow force field blocking me." I swallowed hard, eyebrows furrowing. "It definitely wasn't fairy magic. It was different."

"Stronger?"

I shook my head, more than a little offended by the question. "Just different."

Supernaturals loved to play the comparison game: see who was stronger, faster, more magically inclined. Nobody understood that everyone's abilities served a purpose. We were all powerful in our own right. Nobody was *superior.* That was what snobs like Jasmine didn't understand. Nobody was *better.* We were just *different.*

Somehow rationalizing that made me feel better.

"Different how?"

"I don't know." I shrugged, though my shoulders didn't feel attached to my body anymore. Everything sagged, limp, as the adrenaline started to fade and I suddenly felt drained. "I couldn't pierce through the magic. It wasn't nature-based, that's for sure. More like..." I inhaled sharply, as an almost unfathomable idea came to mind, and Darius's features morphed from curious to confused when I glared up at him. "Did you tell anyone you were helping me?"

He uttered something close to a petulant scoff. "Wouldn't be a very good bodyguard if I just shouted all my clients' names from the rooftops—"

"Because I think," I pressed, growing stronger as the accusation formulated in my head, "that you let it slip, and somehow your *witch* ex—"

"Don't be fucking ridiculous—"

"Caught wind that you were helping me—"

"She's not *that* petty as to—"

"She took away your wings!" I shouted again, catching my back on the corner of the TV as I shot up. Biting back a wince, I squared my shoulders and kept a level, even stare. "Your jealous witch ex-girlfriend just sent a freaking gargoyle to kill me. *That's* why I couldn't see inside the package. I've got a lot of abilities as a fairy, but a witch's spell can be almost impossible to break through. You know that yourself."

"Ravena punished me because I wronged her," Darius argued, not rising to my volume just yet. He seemed to mull it over for a few seconds, and just as he was about to speak, there was a knock at my door. He held up a hand to stop me from investigating right away, then beckoned me over, silently, and had me look through the peephole.

*Josie.* Typical. The woman next door had nothing to do all day while her husband was at work, so between soap operas, she liked sticking her nose in my business.

Pushing Darius out of the way, I hastily unlocked everything and poked my head out. "Hi, Josie."

"Is everything okay in there?" She tried to peer around me, but I wasn't giving her much space to snoop.

"Yeah. Everything's fine."

"I heard a crash—"

"I had an accident," I blurted. "Stumbled into the, uh, balcony door, and..."

"Accident doing *what?*" Her lips slipped into a knowing smirk when heat rose to my cheeks. "Oh. Oh, I see. Well. Never mind then."

*Great.* Now she thought I had aggressive enough sex to actually break our stupidly thick, totally weather-proofed sliding doors. I smiled in a sort of aw-shucks-you-caught-me kind of way, then said a quick goodbye, my tone nicer than she deserved. My smile dropped the second she was gone, toddling back to her apartment like she had the grandest secret in all the universe, and I shut the door harder than necessary.

"Ravena wouldn't come after *you*," Darius told me as I picked my way through the mess back to the living room, resuming the conversation where we'd left off. "She doesn't need to punish you. You're blameless in all this."

"Jealous women tend not to see it that way."

"Aren't all witches that... rah-rah girl power thing?" he asked, wiggling out a pathetic excuse for jazz hands as I stared at him, fists planted on my hips. "No?"

"That's a rather broad brush to paint with," I told him dully. "The heart does crazy things to people, no matter how feminist your leanings."

"She couldn't..."

"There isn't even the *slightest* possibility?" I gestured to my destroyed living room, then to the pile of crumbled stone at our feet. "That thing was encased in magic. Mages are more earth-based. Fae can't cast spells on a whim. It *had* to be the work of a witch. There's no other super out there who fits this MO."

I noticed the flicker of his jaw as he clenched and unclenched it. Darius then crouched down and sifted through the destroyed gargoyle, expression bleak.

"I guess there is a...possibility—"

I threw my hands up in the air. "*Thank you.*"

"A very *slight* possibility," Darius added as he stood back up, dusting his hands off on his jeans. He looked at me with that cocky grin on his face that told me he wasn't willing to concede just yet. "I think the best thing to do is to just confront her about it, and find out if you're right."

"Huh? Do you really think that's the best idea?" This woman just tried to have me squished to goo in my own apartment. Was storming the witch's castle really such a good idea? Was it our only idea? I cocked my head to the side, studying him from a new perspective, as my brain switched gears from confused fairy to clinical psychologist. "Have you seen her since she took your wings?"

He scratched at the back of his neck and avoided my gaze.

"I'll take that as a no." Slowly massaging my temples, I headed for my couch and collapsed onto it after pushing some fallen picture frames out of the way. "Are you even ready to confront her now? Is it a healthy time for you?"

"I don't give a fuck if it's *healthy* for me," he snapped, though clearly, I'd struck a nerve with the way he started pacing again. "You're in danger, potentially because of me. My feelings don't matter."

"Of course they do."

"No—"

"They matter to me." If this Ravena witch *was* the danger Darius sensed, then this whole situation was a lot more manageable than either of us thought. *If* I was right, then we were just dealing with a jealous ex. The problem was mundane—though made a little more challenging by throwing magic into the mix. But I could handle mundane. I'd talked clients through more break-ups and their messy aftermaths than I cared to admit. If Ravena was behind all this because she was bitter about Darius showering me with his unwavering—slightly unnerving—attention, then we could dial things back a notch and take a deep breath.

The danger wasn't quite as serious as my dragon had made it out to be, but I didn't want him getting his heart torn to pieces in the process. It hardly seemed fair.

"I can handle Ravena," he told me as he stood in front of my balcony, a warm summer afternoon breeze rolling in. "She might have taken my wings, but I'm still a dragon. I'm not afraid of her."

"Fear wasn't exactly what I was referring to, but okay," I said, sighing. "When do you want to leave?"

"As soon as possible." He kicked at a huge chunk of broken door, then glanced over his shoulder at me. "But first... we should probably see about getting your shit in order."

I flopped back on the couch with a groan and closed my eyes tight.

TWO DAYS LATER WE WERE ON THE ROAD. DESPITE BOTH OF US wanting to get this little witch problem sorted out right away, both Darius and I agreed we needed to pump the brakes, but for different reasons. I needed to get my clients sorted out if I planned to be away for a few days, which meant I had to update Karen on all their information and make sure she was ready to take over while I was gone. Those patients who weren't comfortable seeing Karen—for one reason or another—had to be referred to other psychologists in the city, of which there were only a few that were comfortable taking clients on at the last second. So, while I spent two days calling around and rearranging appointments, Darius used the time to clean up my apartment, and - as he insisted - get my shit in order.

The door was the first thing to be replaced. He hired a cleaning crew to come in and clear out any woefully unsalvageable furniture, along with the dust of the defeated gargoyle. No one ever asked what the hell had happened, though I knew they wanted to from the looks on their faces whenever they passed by.

As predicted, my superintendent flipped his lid over all the damage. Given that my unit was a rental, my security deposit was *gone*, used strictly for the smaller repairs while I offered to shoulder the fees of the larger ones. At one point, my superintendent even asked if I wanted to file a police report. He'd looked from Darius to me and back again. At the time, Darius had been barking orders on the phone about getting the door delivery guys there by the end of the day—I assume he thought there had been a domestic dispute between us.

"No," I'd insisted, trying not to laugh. "That really isn't necessary."

I probably didn't persuade him much, but at least he'd stopped asking.

Once everything in my life was back in some semblance of an order, I packed a bag and picked Darius up in my iron-free car—custom-made in Alfheim, of course—and we left the city. Once over the bridges, we switched spots, since Darius knew the best route to get to his ex's, and I got to enjoy a little downtime as a passenger.

Even though we were on our way to meet the person who had stolen Darius's greatest joy—and essentially alienated him from his shifter clan—he'd been in a remarkably good mood. Apparently, he really enjoyed driving.

"It's like flying," he'd noted when I commented on his chipper mood, to which I'd snorted and rolled my eyes.

"Doubt it."

We fought over the radio stations, stopped for lunch at a rest-stop burger joint, and took a short walk through the forest at one point, just to stretch our legs and get some fresh air. It was *almost* like we were on an ordinary road trip, and not, you know, making our way to a witch's castle to confront her about whether she sent a gargoyle to kill me, or not. For a few hours, here and there, it all seemed very *normal*— with great conversation, tunes jacked up, and Darius not acting like an over-protective ass.

That was, until we pulled up to Ravena's front gates and he rolled down the window so he could reach a keypad that I assumed would give us access.

"What do you mean I have to stay in the car?" I demanded, arms crossed and lower lip pushed out in a childish pout. He ignored me, punching in the numerical code on the keypad. When something buzzed, he poked his head out the window and waved at a camera. Seconds later, the wrought iron gates started to swing open.

We had driven north, for the most part, a pretty straight shot from the city, and were now in the wilds of north New York state. Ravena had one of those old manors, the kind you'd see in sweeping period dramas with British royalty, though the unkempt ivy and piles of old, upswept leaves from last fall, kind of took the charm away. While the house was sprawling, and enclosed in a ten-foot wall, it kind of just looked dirty and old, in need of a serious cleansing rain.

I'd always thought being a witch meant your house would be spotless, but as I peered through the dashboard, lip curled, I quickly decided that wasn't the case. I mean, couldn't you just use a spell and keep everything clean? I'd kill for that kind of power. Scrubbing my apartment top to bottom, every weekend, absolutely sucked.

"I mean," Darius said when he stopped my car in the middle of the cobblestone courtyard and put it into park, "you have to wait here. I don't know how she'll react to me bringing another woman into her home."

"Oh, yeah, she totally didn't sic a gargoyle after me," I grumbled, arms crossed as I slumped into my seat. "And here I was, ready to share some power with you. Maybe I'll just send you in blind."

He turned the car off with a sigh, then unbuckled his seatbelt and faced me. "What are you whining about?"

I scowled, though I sensed a nugget of truth behind his words. He was probably right, after all, about leaving me behind. Was I the kind of person Ravena would invite into her home—the random fairy who showed up with her ex-boyfriend, probably covered in his scent after spending the last few days together?

*Could witches scent that kind of stuff?* I'd always wondered...

I shook my head as my thoughts started to wander. "Sorry. You're right."

"I know I'm right." The smirk didn't help soothe my temper, though. I ignored it pointedly, and instead reached a hand out and swatted his shoulder. "Get going."

"Going," He handed me the keys and opened the door. "I won't leave until she agrees to help us."

I nodded as he got out and slammed the door. "Let's hope she will."

❧ 6 ❧

JUST BECAUSE I wasn't allowed in the sprawling TV worthy manor didn't mean I'd be content to sit in the car like a scolded child. Once I watched Darius disappear inside the front doors, I grabbed my purse and slipped out of the car. While the transfer of my powers to him had left me a little woozy, I managed to dart across the courtyard, lightning quick, courtesy of fae speed, and crouch down in the shrubs—shrubs in desperate need of a trimming.

*Seriously.* What was the point of being a witch if you didn't keep your house and garden immaculate? I winced when some of the branches dug into me, but the pain was worth it. Fairies had a number of extra-sensory gifts that we could whip out when we wanted, and tuck away when they weren't needed. I couldn't imagine walking around this world, or any other, with my super-sonic hearing abilities turned up at all times. I'd go insane. But for now, with a little coaxing and a dollop of white magic use, I was able to crank up the volume and listen in on what was being said inside the house.

Of course, I'd really only be able to hear what was happening in the foyer and whatever other rooms were nearby. If they retreated into some dingy dungeon two floors down, Darius was on his own. But at the sound of heeled shoes clicking toward the front door, I knew this would be good enough for now.

"Darius." I stiffened at the sound of Ravena's voice, but only because it sounded like it was *right* beside me. This was what happened when you didn't use your senses all that often; it could get a little overwhelming, just as my extra sight made me dizzy when I'd tried to peer inside the gargoyle box.

"Ravena." He sounded tense, like he was speaking through tight lips. I exhaled deeply, wondering still if this had been a good idea. Was he ready to face her? Could he be my advocate if he was wrapped up in drama with his ex?

We were about to find out.

"Look, I'm not here to catch up on the good times, or rehash the bad," he all but sneered after a tense beat had passed. I rolled my eyes. Even though he had as much a reason as any to be a dick to a witch, we needed her help. If she wasn't responsible for my attack—unlikely—then we could use her help to find out who *was* behind it.

"Good times? Bad? I think you mean downright ugly. I have no good memories left of you, Darius." She hissed.

"I'm sorry to hear that, Ravena. But again, I'm not here to talk about us."

"Oh, of course, you aren't. I assume you came to barter over the use of your wings," she fired back, her voice low—seductive? I made a face. *Ugh.* She had the voice of a seasoned smoker, but if she snagged a guy like Darius, I had to assume she had the looks to counteract that throaty, crackly rumble.

"I'm not here for me," Darius told her, still stiff. "I need to know if you commanded a gargoyle to attack a friend of mine. A fae."

"The one you left me for?" My eyes widened, and I swore my heart skipped a beat. Ravena gave a cold chuckle. "No. I did nothing to her, despite the insults she paid me. How is your paramour, anyway?"

In the lengthy bout of silence that followed, I almost thought I'd lost my connection inside. Wiggling a finger in my ear, I leaned in closer, frowning, until...

"She left."

Ravena burst out into a cruel, mocking laughter, the kind that told me his heartbreak vindicated her own.

"Serves you right, dragon." She spat out the words.

"Enough, Ravena," Darius replied, his voice filled with impatience. "Did you, or did you not, send a gargoyle after a fae? I've been working with her because I sense the danger around her, and then this gargoyle shows up, and—"

She scoffed. "Gargoyles aren't really my thing. I thought you'd know that."

"I do," he noted quickly, and I heard the earnestness in his voice. Surely Ravena did as well. "I just had to be sure. The gargoyle was sent to her wrapped in witch's magic. Since she doesn't know any witches personally, we came to you. Not because I think you're capable of sending an assassin after someone, but because... I'd hoped you might help us."

"And why would I ever want to help you?" Although she had tried to sound tough, the witch's voice wavered slightly, and I could imagine her crossing her arms—defensive, hurt. Darius affected her more than she would ever care to admit; I could tell that just by listening to her speak.

"Ravena, you know why." I heard some footsteps. "Please. A woman's life is in danger. If you didn't send the gargoyle—"

"You know I didn't." There was that hurt again, slowly edging out the anger and bitterness. I almost felt bad for accusing her of the crime in the first place.

*Almost.*

"Then we need to find out who did," Darius said, finally sounding like he had control over the situation. "I'm not asking for me. I'm asking so this woman doesn't get hurt. That's all."

"Are you two involved?"

"We're just friends."

I bit my lip as a stab of hurt shot through me. It wasn't fair to feel that way. Just because I wanted to get him into bed didn't mean we were a thing. I had no ownership over Darius, and, honestly, if I had to make the choice, I'd rather have his friendship than some weird romantic thing that would probably crash and burn anyway.

The conversation went mute for a little while again, and I made myself more comfortable in the bushes, twitching whenever the spiny branches poked me. It took so long for her to make up her mind that I debated going back to sit in the car with the AC blasting, but in the end, Ravena conceded.

"Wait here," she ordered softly, and I leaned in closer as her footfalls faded. Moments later she was back. "My black mirror will show all things. I'll need a drop of blood to—"

"Of course you do," Darius grumbled. A sharp intake of air followed, and I made a face at the sound of droplets hitting a hard surface—presumably the blood offering on the mirror's surface. I owed him one. Blood magic wasn't something many played around with: not without serious consideration, anyway.

"Now take my hand."

"Ravena—"

"Just do it," she snapped. I bit back a laugh. Apparently, all the women in Darius's life handled his alpha bullshit by yelling at him.

"So, what do you see?"

"Give it a moment." She sounded more impatient than him. "I see the box. I see the magic. You were right in assuming it was witch's magic."

"Kaye figured that out, actually."

I tensed at the use of my name, but no one else seemed to care.

"It's a man... A warlock," Ravena continued, followed swiftly by a sharp gasp. "Abramelin!"

"Abra-what?"

"A dangerous and very powerful warlock," Ravena replied hastily. "He is not one you ought to tangle with."

"Trust me, Kaye isn't the type of person to tangle with anyone. She works all the time, keeps to herself." He had a fair point there. Not only did I have no idea who this Abramelin person was, but I was too busy in my day-to-day existence to stir up any sort of drama with a warlock. Clearly, I was the target of a hate crime—or a case of mistaken identity.

"He enchanted the box," the witch said. The way she said it —the words created a heavy knot in my gut, one that made me want to take off running. I was very quickly getting way in over my head.

"Do you know why?"

"The mirror only shows who," Ravena insisted, "not the why. Speaking of who…" Her voice suddenly thundered in my ears, and I tumbled out of the bushes with a yelp. "You may enter my home, fairy. No point in hiding in my shrubbery anymore."

I wriggled a finger in each ear, trying to rid them of the high-pitched whine that followed her invite. When the sudden bout of tinnitus finally ebbed, me popping my jaw and blinking hard like an idiot, I scrambled to my feet and made my way for the front door.

"She saw you in the mirror, apparently," Darius said, sounding somewhat apologetic when he opened the door for me. I glowered up at him, then flinched out of the way when he reached for my head. He shot me a look, and with an annoyed huff I stood there and let him pick the twigs out of my hair. *Perfect.* The shifter smirked, head cocked slightly to one side. "Pretty sure I told you to wait in the car."

"Pretty sure I don't take orders from you," I snapped, though I forced a little half-smile when a flicker of hurt washed over his features. There was something unsaid with what I'd snapped —*shifter*. Like I didn't take orders from the lesser. It wasn't my intention, but I was sure this wasn't the first time someone had sneered it at him in the supernatural community. Tucking my wild hair behind my ears, I cleared my throat and nodded toward the interior of the manor. "Come on. Introduce me to your ex already. I'm on pins and needles."

I noticed his hesitation in the way he hovered by the front door as if blocking me from whatever lay in wait beyond. Rolling my eyes, I shoved by and made my way in, knowing that I had to face Ravena one way or another. She stood waiting for me in the grand foyer with a cathedral ceiling and a dusty glass chandelier overhead. I hoped my surprise didn't show, but she looked nothing as I'd expected. Tall. Lanky. Her hair had a straw-like dry quality to it, even at a distance, and wavered somewhere between mousy brown and dirty blonde. Her eyes, a deep green, were quite lovely. Almost the same color as mine.

I'd thought she would be a bombshell if she managed to land a guy as gorgeous as Darius. In fact, I'd assumed she would be stunning simply because she was a witch. After all, spells and potions and charms could be crafted to energize one's vitality and youth. Ravena, however, looked much older than I had expected, and when she offered a faint smile, her dark green gaze studying me in silence, I noted the way her skin crinkled around her eyes.

In that moment, I firmly reminded myself I ought not to judge physical appearances. After all, I wasn't exactly the typical image of a fairy either. Most fae looked like Catriona and Jasmine. I was an anomaly. Ravena was probably thinking the exact same thing about me, as I was about her.

*How did she land Darius?*

*Weren't fairies supposed to be pretty and thin?*

I squared my shoulders and decided to be the bigger person.

"It's nice to meet you," I managed, as I extended my hand. Even if I wasn't feeling it, I could slip into my work-Kaye persona pretty easily when I was around people I didn't click with right away. "I'm Kaye Allister. I'm a friend of Darius's."

The door closed gently behind me, but I faced forward, offering Ravena my full attention, as Darius moved back to my side.

"Ravena," the witch offered. She took my hand in hers, and at the slightest feel of her magical essence, I steeled myself with a surge of white magic.

A flicker of surprise passed across her face, something you'd miss if you blinked. I wanted to establish quickly that while I might not have been a witch, I was a magical being in my own right, and my white magic was limitless. Easily depleted if used too much, of course, but it always returned. A fairy's white magic was like walking around with an invisible coat of armor; sure, it wouldn't protect you from a knife or a gun, but when called upon, it could befuddle an attacker, or temporarily block harmful spells and influences.

Ravena had clearly been testing the waters, and when our clasped hands fell apart, I felt as though we separated on relatively even footing.

As even as one could get in a stranger's home. The witch would always have the upper hand here. I bolstered my white magic for good measure, deciding I'd crash in the car once we left and recover there.

"So," I said in the incredibly tense silence that followed. I could feel both Ravena and Darius staring right through me—the witch glaring daggers, the dragon looking...concerned? Both were super unnecessary. Rolling my shoulders back, I pushed on, sliding my psychologist mask into place. "You saw a warlock in your mirror?"

"The warlock who cast the spell on your stone visitor, yes," Ravena told me, her arms crossed. "Abramelin."

"The name isn't familiar to me."

"It wouldn't be," the witch mused, lips twitching into a smirk. "We all tend to know our own kind. Abramelin is an ArchMage."

*ArchMage*—leader of a coven of Warlocks and Witches. *Holy shit*. I shifted my weight side to side, mulling the information over. As far as I knew, I hadn't done anything recently to piss off a coven.

"Well, at no point have we been introduced," I insisted with a quick glance at Darius to see if he believed me. When I lifted my eyebrows slightly, he gave a small nod. With a sigh, I faced Ravena again. "Nor do I get involved in politics, or anything dangerous within our world. Did you see anything specific in that mirror of yours?"

The black mirror hung from a black lace strand attached to her belt. Her dress, an unsightly pale purple, gave her the illusion of lacking a figure.

She pursed her lips for a moment. "No."

"You sure?"

"Positive."

"Ravena," Darius said, and I didn't miss the way heat bloomed in her cheeks. "Come on. Anything you can tell us that will help Kaye live to see her next birthday will be useful."

"Charming," I muttered, shooting him a quick look.

"Just as you profess not to involve yourself in the politics of our world, I too have no desire to tangle with a warlock as powerful as Abramelin." Ravena picked at her nails to give the impression of nonchalance, but I could spot the awkwardness in her movements a mile away. She wasn't a disinterested bitch by nature. Darius must have brought out that side in her, and I briefly contemplated sending the shifter back to wait in the car. Maybe it would have been easier for just Ravena and I to hash this thing out on our own.

"Is there anything you can recommend to protect ourselves?" Darius pressed, sounding a bit more frustrated with every word uttered. I glanced back at Ravena, wondering what kind of tone might make her snap. She studied Darius with a veiled look, then swallowed hard and flicked her hand toward a staircase. There was a dusty set that went up to another floor paired with one that went down to the basement.

"I have some protection bags in my workshop," she noted, "along with a few charmed runes and crystals to keep intruders out of your space. I'd use them in your car, your home. It won't solve the problem, but it will beef up your defenses."

Darius gave a curt nod before jogging toward the stairs, disappearing down the one that led to the lower levels of the house. Once he was gone, it was less tense between the Witch and I than I'd expected—but not by much.

"You know, you ought to be careful around him," she said, as we both continued to stare at each other, like some weird magical Western standoff, though neither of us had a gun on our hip.

Well, I suppose we each had metaphorical guns.

"I'm just trying not to get killed by some asshole warlock," I assured her.

"Good." She tried to flick her hair over her shoulder, but it lacked the glossy shimmer that would make the gesture effective. "He's a heartbreaker."

"I heard." With a nod, I tightened my psychologist mask in place. "And you're a wing-taker."

"That was warranted."

"Because he left you?"

"Because I found his loyalty lacking," she said sharply, eyes flashing. "When he learns to be selfless, to love another as much as he loves his own precious ego, then he will have his wings returned."

"So you're here to give life lessons?"

"No." Her cheeks flushed a dull red that made her complexion look ashy. "I merely wanted to spare the next hapless woman who fell for his charms a little pain. Darius has led an easy, carefree life. He toyed with my heart and tossed it aside like it was nothing. He needed to learn—"

"Suffering?" I suggested, to which she pressed her lips together for a moment and scowled.

"He needed to learn to be *human*." The Witch sniffed, the rhythm of our conversation broken when she turned away, muttering, "I can think of many creatures in our world who could do with learning the same lesson."

Even though I merely pressed my lips together and turned away when Ravena lifted her green eyes to mine, searching them for a reaction, I had to agree with her. There were plenty of stuffy supernaturals in our secret magical world who could learn a thing or two from the most mundane species around. Humans were... *trying*. They could be a nuisance. A pest. A bore. But at least they lived their lives to the fullest—or at least most did. Love 'em or hate 'em, you had to respect them. They loved and lost, and fought for every breath of their, what, eighty or ninety years on Earth? No one besides vampires and demons—that I knew of, anyway—was immortal. Fae were gifted with longer lives, but only by another fifty or sixty years. Witches could prolong their lifetime with potions when brewed successfully, but eventually, they too would die.

We all laughed in the face of Mother Nature, and Father Time, here and there as supernaturals. Humans just had to *be*. They had to fight. They had to exist. They had to carve out a spot in their cruel, magicless, mundane world, or they'd fade into nothing.

In many ways, they were a stronger race than us supernaturals.

I could see why Ravena might want to knock an arrogant shifter down a peg or two by making him experience the more *human* side of things, especially concerning matters of the heart. Still, in no way, shape, or form did I want to appear as though I condoned her actions, or agreed with her behavior. Cursing a shifter – a dragon shifter, at that – with the inability to use his wings and fly was outright heartless. Not to mention, dangerous to that shifter's existence when flying was one of the basic, and natural ways they knew to evade enemies. I didn't care how bitter, or heartbroken she was, that was just wrong.

So, I stayed silent, instead observing the architectural and design elements around Ravena's dusty, though sparse home. If you got rid of the grime that seemed to exist in every corner of the room, and gave the scuffed floors a good scrubbing, this place could really shine.

For now, it was a bit like Ravena: sad, desperate and abandoned. I bit my lower lip to keep from reaching out to her, or encouraging her to open up to me. I wasn't here as a therapist, no matter how deeply my heart yearned to stop the suffering, and help her through the pain that she was obviously feeling. I was here for one reason, and one reason only: to find out who was after me, and now that I had, there were far more pressing matters to deal with. Namely, trying to figure out how to stop them before they killed me.

Yes, this desperate Witch, and her broken heart would have to seek an outlet somewhere else. After all, an ArchMage was looking for me. He'd singled me out for some reason, and I had to figure out why, and how to put an end to it – before it was too late.

I crossed my arms, and I knew what that body language would mean to her: I wasn't interested, or engaging her. In truth, it was just to comfort myself, more than anything, pushing back the anxiety and the steadily rising fear by pressing tighter and tighter until it all went away—for now.

Footsteps thundered up the stairs just as I heard Ravena draw another breath, and we both whirled around to find Darius returning. He had a small gray bag, like the bags you'd see dollar bills on in cartoons, that looked on the verge of bursting, but I didn't comment. If Ravena had a bunch of magical crap that would protect us, then we were taking as much with us, as she was willing to part with. She raised a hand when Darius tried to breeze by, then rooted through the bag as he stood there, scowling. The Witch plucked two crystals from the bag, and shoved them into her pockets, leaving the rest to us.

"There is a magical village in this world," she told us as Darius returned to my side. I resisted the urge to clamp a hand down on his arm to wordlessly communicate that I was ready to get the hell out of here. Somehow the gesture seemed too obvious. Ravena's face, however, seemed tinged with sadness at our impending departure. "It is a shifter clan with the odd Witch and Warlock. The glyphs on its town sign will spell *Aerath* when you use the appropriate rune stone. You won't find trouble there, though the clan is secretive, they are relatively peaceful, once they determine friend from foe."

"As most shifters are," Darius muttered, and I shrugged when our eyes met. He didn't have to convince *me*. I wasn't the one who thought all shifters were bloodthirsty mongrels that didn't deserve to co-exist with the rest of us; that was Jasmine's game.

"Look for a mage there who goes by the name of Noris," Ravena instructed us. "He trained Abramelin in his youth, and knows him better than anyone. He may have some insight as to how best to defeat him."

My eyebrows shot up. "Thank you, Ravena. That's... That's very helpful."

She gave a demure nod, one I returned before saying goodbye, and making a beeline for the door. Behind me, Darius followed at a slower clip.

"Ravena, I really appreciate all this," I heard him say as I opened the door. "Now, I can't go without asking... Any chance you could reverse the curse? Maybe give me my wings back now that I'm going up against the leader of a coven?"

She issued a laugh that almost sounded genuine, and I glanced back, my hand on the doorknob, and caught her offering a watery smile.

"You know I can't do that, Darius."

"Come on—"

"Because I made sure the spell could only be lifted by you

fulfilling the requirements." She cocked her head to the side, eyes only for Darius, and sighed. "I knew I might give in one day, if you asked nicely enough so I made sure that even I couldn't break the spell. You know me, Darius. I can't seem to ever say no to you."

*Right. Time to go.* I held back the urge to roll my eyes, and hurried for the car.

## 7

BEFORE WE LEFT Ravena's home, both Darius and I realized we had basically nothing to work with as far as finding this magical shifter village where Abramelin's former mentor lived. So, while I'd waited in the car, Darius ducked back inside to get a bit more information.

"Just ask for the fucking directions," I'd told him, eager to get going and assuming he'd go in and give the Witch attitude. "Get in, and get out."

And, despite his growling at me, my dragon companion did as he was told. Less than ten minutes later he'd been back in the car by my side, with a sticky-note gift for me—and all the detailed directions available for us to follow. We ended up driving all the way to Vermont and into the state's wild interior. By the time we reached the town sign, it was dark, and both of us were exhausted.

"I don't know about you," Darius said after rubbing at his eyes, head resting on the seat and expression world-weary, "but I don't have it in me to go compare dick sizes with a bunch of bear shifters tonight."

"Generally I try to avoid dick comparisons." I lowered the radio, and then started fishing through Ravena's bag of magic stones and charm pouches. "But I see your point." I glanced up for a moment, frowning. "*Bear* shifters?"

"Yeah," Darius chuckled, a genuine sound I hadn't heard since before we reached his ex's house. "they can be pretty testy when provoked."

"Right. Don't poke the bear," I mused, nodding. "What sage advice I've never before heard in my whole life—"

"Hah," he muttered dryly. "Let's find a place to hunker down for the night."

My lips twitched; I'd never wanted to jump on the term *hunker down* so badly before, but I was just too tired for teasing.

"Wait. I want to confirm the sign."

I searched through the rune stones to find the one with the carvings I knew indicated a second sight of sorts. Just as Ravena had said, the town's sign was scrawled in glyphs—carved into the wood. I almost thought we were on a native reservation, but the glyphs looked more European—Russian, actually—than local. So, clenching my fist around the rune stone, a magenta stone about half the size of my palm, I connected its innate magical properties with a surge of my white magic. Sure enough, the letters rearranged themselves into English—until I loosened my fist.

"Aerath," I told him. "Ravena led us in the right direction."

"I knew she would." He shrugged when I shot him a slightly narrowed look. "Well... I'd *hoped*."

We pulled away from the sign, both agreeing it'd be best to try to enter this secret magical village in daylight. Both of us were tired from driving all day, anyway. Neither of us wanted to fight security, be it the magical kind or just the brute strength kind, when we felt like this. While darkness offered better sleuthing opportunities, we were in Aerath to ask for help. No one would want to help two outsiders who snuck in during the dead of night. It wouldn't exactly strike the right chord with anyone.

After discovering all the nearby motels were full, we turned the car around and headed for the nearest conservation area. Sure enough, we were able to snag a camping spot from the poor guy on overnight duty at the park's front desk. Although we considered just pulling off on the side of the road and starting a fire, it seemed safer to be somewhere with other people around. Yeah, the gargoyle attacked me in a building *full* of people, but if it meant I could sleep easier, Darius seemed more inclined to go with it.

After settling our fees, we drove into the park to our designated spot. Amongst the trees was a rounded spot, clearly intended for tent pitching and fire starting. While we had no tent to pitch, the seats of my hatchback folded down nicely enough, and while Darius got a fire going, I set up our sleeping arrangements for the night.

Well, I set up mine. Darius pointedly reminded me that *he* was on duty when I'd asked him if he preferred the left, or right, side of the bed.

*Whatever.*

Once I'd spread out some car blankets and folded a few articles of clothing to make a pillow, I went around the parameter of our campsite planting Ravena's protection crystals. I gave each one an infusion of white magic, lifting my hands up and over so that the magic would connect over our campsite, like a bubble. It didn't provide the invisibility that a ward would, but since I couldn't make one without the help of my fae sisters, this was the best we could do. If someone tried to breach my white magic barrier, I'd feel it in my bones—even if I was dead asleep.

We'd stopped for fast food on the way, so while we unpacked our burgers and fries, sharing a log that Darius had dragged out of the woods in front of the fire, I studied him out of the corner of my eye. After a while, he sighed, a bit too dramatically.

"What, Kaye?"

I shrugged as I stuffed some fries in my mouth. I seldom ate out unless I was in Alfheim, and usually needed to bolster myself with my white magic so I could manage any iron in the food.

Since my white magic was running low, I could already feel the sickly churn of my stomach with every bite. But I was starving. And fries were delicious.

"Just curious," I said, after I swallowed that mouthful.

"About?"

"The woman you left Ravena for." There was no point in beating around the bush. If we were going to work together to get Abramelin off my tail, we needed to be honest with each other. Honest and straightforward.

"What d'you want to know?" he said, words muffled by a mouthful of burger. I bit down on my inner lip for a few seconds; I *knew* I had to be straightforward, but sometimes it was easier said than done. He sighed again, this time with his lips curved into a grin. "*Kaye*. Speak now, or forever hold your fucking peace."

"I was listening to your conversation with Ravena... out in the bushes—"

"*Kaye*—"

I snorted. "Like I was seriously just going to sit in the car. Anyway." I ignored the glare he shot me. "I heard her asking about the fairy you left her for. Is it true? Did you leave her for a fairy?"

While there was no sigh again, he didn't answer right away. Instead, I watched him play with his food before eating it, the playful smirk from thirty seconds ago, long gone.

"Yeah," Darius muttered when I cleared my throat pointedly. "Yeah, she was a fairy."

"So, do you have, like, a *type* or something?"

"It just happened," he told me, my teasing smile doing nothing to chase the bitterness out of his voice. "I'd never even met a fairy before Jas, not personally anyway. I thought she was the most beautiful creature I'd ever seen. Took me a little while to realize she had a pretty outer shell, and a rotten core."

"Sweet on the outside, sour on the inside." I rolled my eyes. "Sounds like a few fairies I know."

Darius offered a weak chuckle in return while I set my dinner aside, unable to fend off the iron in the food any longer—not until my white magic regenerated, anyway. Feeling slightly nauseous, I placed a hand to my sweaty forehead, and watched the fire until a thought occurred to me.

"Wait. What did you say her name was?"

"Jas—"

"Jas?" I let the name roll around in my head for a bit, frowning. "Is that her full name? Is she local?"

I assumed she'd be a NYC gal like me if that was where Darius had lived while he dated her, and I didn't know any fae that went by the name of Jas.

"Well, *Jasmine*," he clarified, after another too big bite. My nausea took off, full force, and I swallowed down the bile creeping up my throat. "She lives in state, but not in the city. She—"

"I know her," I said stiffly, and out of the corner of my eye I saw his head swivel toward me.

"Ah. I can tell just by your tone that we share an opinion of her."

My lips tried to twist into a smile at the sound of him chuckling, but that failed miserably. I didn't have a right to be bitter or jealous or whatever—but Jasmine was the literal worst fairy I could think of. Darius seemed like a nice guy, for the most part. Yeah, a little intense, but it was probably a dragon thing. He absolutely didn't deserve to go from having his wings removed by his witch ex, to probably having his balls hacked off by Jasmine. I couldn't even fathom what kind of relationship they'd had, even if he'd already shared some details.

"Yeah, she's... She's not my favorite person," I remarked coolly, gaze fixed on the fire, my mouth set in a thin line. Darius took the hint for once and let it be, eating the rest of his meal in silence, as the fire crackled before us.

*Jasmine.* Seriously?!

I closed my eyes and concentrated on my breathing, willing

the swirling sick feeling in my gut to fade. I knew it was the iron —for the most part—but learning about Jasmine hadn't helped. As I sat there, my ass growing more and more numb on the unrelentingly hard wood beneath it, Jasmine's words at our fairy sister retreat earlier in the month flashed back to me. She'd been so cruel talking about shifters, so cold and callous. She had even mentioned that she'd dated one in the past—and made it out like he'd been a dog. Darius didn't deserve to be treated like that.

Well, if I didn't hate Jasmine before, I certainly did now.

And *not* because she and Darius had dated.

Just because she was an awful person.

Okay, maybe a *little* because she had dated Darius, but that was because she had been so horrible when she told us about him. I'd never be able to look at her the same again.

*What a bitch!*

"Hey, you okay?" I flinched when Darius's hand gently pressed down on my shoulder. "You're shaking."

"It's the iron in the food," I said, perhaps a little too quickly, and motioned to my bag of uneaten fast food. "Normally I can use my white magic to fend it off, but I used a lot today already."

"Oh. Shit. Fuck. I didn't even think about that." He crumpled his empty wrappers and tossed them into the fire, then shuffled closer to me. Before I could stop him, an arm wrapped around my shoulders. "What hurts? What can I do to help?"

"Mostly my stomach," I told him, though I had no intentions of sharing the fact that the rest of my digestive system would go through hell too if my white magic didn't bolster soon. After all, the iron was working its way out. Not a pleasant experience— not the kind you'd want to go through in front of a hot guy, anyway. "And there's nothing you can do, unless you've got a reserve of white magic in you somewhere that I could borrow."

"I'd give you all of it, if I could." He shot me a rather sexy smirk-wink combo, then jogged off to the car and returned moments later. "Anything in Ravena's bag that'll help?"

"No," I said quickly, pushing the bag away. "No, it just has to work itself through. My magic will take longer to regenerate while I'm feeling like crap, so I think I'm in for a rough night."

"Fuck. Kaye, I'm sorry. I should have thought—"

"It's not *your* fault," I assured him with a forced smile. "Seriously. I'm a big girl. I should have known this would happen."

I watched him tie off the bag of clattering crystals and runes before setting it aside. He then settled down next to me and started rubbing my back. I was about to tell him not to worry, but it felt *so* good, so soothing, that I just closed my eyes and let him do his thing. His large hand drew random shapes, alternating occasionally between the pads of his fingers and his fingernails. The nails sent shivers down my spine, and soon his touch was all I could concentrate on, leaning in and resting my head on his shoulder.

After a while, the cold sweats stopped. My stomach still ached, but not in the way it had before. But Darius didn't stop. And I didn't ask him to.

Instead, I fell asleep curled up against him, the heat of the fire on my face, and the gentle caress of his touch on my back.

I'd never felt safer in all my life.

## 8

THE STIFFNESS IN MY BACK, legs, and hips the following morning felt worth it, if it meant waking up next to Darius. We'd spent the whole night in front of the fire, me sleeping, and him standing watch—with me in his arms, of course. My whole back-seat bed getup was for naught. After strolling down to the conservation park's toilets for a quick refresh in the privacy of a stall—hello hygiene enchantment, I seldom ever needed you—I was back at our campsite and Darius was packing up. Dark bags surrounded his eyes, but he assured me he'd perk up after his first cup of coffee of the day.

I stood back, letting him do his thing, arms crossed and lips twisted in a concerned frown. Was I pushing him too hard here? Was it too much to ask that he stand watch night and day? We had my white magic shielding us last night, so, really, he could have fallen asleep for a little while. Power napped. *Something.* The whole point of choosing the park over a random spot in the hillside was because we'd assumed this would be safer.

*Stubborn bastard just wouldn't let up.*

So, to accommodate for the fact that he was operating on barely any sleep, I took over the driving duties and paid for our breakfast at a twenty-four-hour diner a half hour from the

Aerath village sign. When we finished, my dragon *did* look a little better, but not by much. A shower would probably do him some good, but he waved off my offer to use a hygiene enchantment on him, too.

"I don't smell that bad."

"If by 'that bad' you mean like a rotten carcass of a skunk after a week in the sun, then sure, you're fine," I told him flatly. I then watched as he rolled layer after layer of deodorant on his armpits under his black t-shirt, maintaining eye contact with me as he did it. When he was through, he capped the deodorant stick, and tossed it in his bag, then slammed the trunk of my car.

"Better?"

"I can still smell you from here," I noted before heading to the driver's side. At least he smelled *better*, though all that deodorant was certainly potent. "I wish you'd just let me enchant you."

"I thought Fairies couldn't do magic." He rolled his eyes and begrudgingly did up his seat belt when I wouldn't take the car out of park until he did.

"We can do magic. Just selective magic," I insisted, backing out of the parking spot and heading for the road. "I guess we're more like mages in that sense. A lot of our power comes from nature, and a lot of spells that don't require intricate incantations usually revolve around manipulating the elements."

I was about to tell him I could summon a thunderstorm with enough concentration—and practice, as I hadn't even attempted the spell in a good decade or so—but stopped short when he chuckled, his lips curving into that smirk I've come to know a little too well.

"I always knew you were all little flowery hippies—"

"I'm hardly *flowery*," I snapped, mildly annoyed when he nodded vehemently in agreement. "And so what if I was? Would it be better if I was just some shifter? More brawn than brain?"

"Hey."

"You started it," I said, sharply. "We all have our stereotypes."

"Some are just worse than others," he muttered before moving on to fiddle with the radio. "I mean, I'd rather be thought of as a flower child, than a moron."

I bit the inside of my cheek. Why did I always do this? I *knew* the whole supernatural vs. shifter thing was a touchy subject for him, yet I let myself toe the line between teasing and seriousness a little too easily. I squared my shoulders, determined to keep a lid on it for the future. The tension managed to lift, thankfully, when a driver in a beat-up pick-up truck zoomed by us, darting into the lane for oncoming traffic rather dramatically before whizzing in front of me—and then slowing down.

I slammed on the horn and flipped him off, letting my New York mouth get the better of me. Darius thought the whole thing was hilarious, and soon enough we were throwing all our tiredness, our stiffness, our weariness, onto the asshole driver in front of us—and the guy, of course, remained in front of us until we turned off onto the barely visible dirt road behind the Aerath village sign.

"Dick," I grumbled, flipping the guy off one last time for good measure.

"If only Abramelin could have seen you now," Darius teased, still chuckling. "I'm sure he'd think twice about coming after you, that's for sure."

I grinned. "If only."

My poor little hatchback only made it another ten minutes through the forest before the road stopped and we had to go on foot. With no village in sight, we packed up our things, me complaining under my breath about over packing my bag, and parked my car off to the side, and hopefully out of sight. I let Darius lead the way, though I took quick stock of the forest as we moved. Quiet. Peaceful. There was a sense of ease within the trees, like they knew they were safe. When the wind rustled through the canopy, the leaves seemed to shimmer with an otherworldly magic that I was only used to seeing in Alfheim. Birds twittered. Squirrels skittered along the branches. Darius's foot caught on the occasional root, but otherwise we moved through the forest unhindered, picking our way through a path —perhaps to nowhere.

Just as I let my mind start to wander, two figures came crashing through the underbrush. Darius swiped me behind, as if to keep me out of the way, and I rolled my eyes. Obviously, I wasn't going to charge toward the pair of meatheads striding toward us. I wasn't *that* oblivious to my own safety.

"You are trespassing on private property," the taller of the two barked. As far as I could tell, neither had any weapons on hand, despite wearing head-to-toe camo. Still, their fists were probably the best weapons at their disposal. I could feel the otherworldliness as they approached, noting that they were most definitely not human.

"We're looking for Aerath," Darius told them, raising his hands slightly, in an effort to look like less of a threat. But if he really wanted to look less intimidating, his hands would have gone all the way up. As it were, he appeared more like he was trying to quiet two raging beasts, than anything else.

"Turn around and head back the way you came," the shorter man ordered. *Shifters.* I wasn't sure how I knew exactly, but I could *feel* it much the same way I could tell a demon and a vampire apart at a distance. I trusted my gut.

"Look, buddy—"

"No, *you* look—"

"Holy shit, Darius?"

My eyebrows knitted together as the whole tone of the conversation shifted. All three men stopped, studying one another. Seconds later they were patting each other on the back like long lost friends.

"Liam... Colton!" I'd never seen my dragon smile as wide as he did in that moment, and I couldn't decide whether that pissed me off or not. "What the hell are you two doing out here?"

"Working security," Liam, the taller of the two, announced.

Made total sense. Both guys certainly *looked* like they were built to protect something or someone. "The village hired us out a while back for the extra muscle. Figured it'd be good money."

Darius nudged him. "And is it?"

Colton shrugged, scratching at his stubble-ridden square jaw. "Could be better."

I crossed my arms, and if I knew Darius could see it, I would have tapped my foot too just for good measure. As the bromance unfolded, and the trio continued back-slapping and joking around, I let out a series of pointed sighs and throat clears that *finally* got Darius's attention.

"Shit, right, sorry." He gestured back to me, and I moved forward as if on cue. "This is Kaye. She's my—"

"Client?" Colton asked, cocking his head to the side as he inspected me a little *too* suggestively.

"Friend," I clarified. While I'd tried to keep the stiffness out of my voice, clearly I'd failed when the meatheads' expressions faltered somewhat. "Darius and I are friends."

"Just like all of us are friends," Darius insisted smoothly, his smile lightening the mood in an instant. "Liam and Colton are from a neighboring shifter clan... Ridgestone. I've known them my whole life. Don't let them fool you, though. They look like grizzlies, but they're more like teddy bears."

Forcing a half-smile, I moved past Darius and extended a hand. "Pleasure to meet you, both."

I'd lose my stiffness once they stopped looking at me like they wanted to lick me from top to bottom. Honestly. Were men so totally oblivious to how obvious they were about their attractions? Fairies were appealing to most supernaturals and shifters, that much I was aware, but it didn't mean I enjoyed the attention by any means.

Liam turned to Darius after shaking my hand, a smile playing on his lips. "I can't believe it's you, man. It's been so long since we've seen you!"

"Yeah, what the hell? Where've you been, and wait, what are

you doing out here?" Colton asked. "Man, aren't you supposed to be taking over for your Dad soon? Figured you'd need some Alpha crash course or something—"

"We're looking for Noris," Darius interjected suddenly, and even though he'd interrupted Colton, I had heard the words perfectly clear.

*Alpha crash course.*

My eyes darted to Darius curiously. *Was my dragon supposed to be an Alpha?*

It would certainly explain the personality quirks. Some of them, anyway.

As the men carried on their discussion, answering Darius's questions about Noris, I tried to listen but found myself sinking deeper and deeper into thought about what I'd heard. Alphas were a big deal in most magical communities. The title wasn't always the same. After all, Abramelin was an "ArchMage" instead of an Alpha, but they basically did the same thing. Run the clan, or coven, or gathering, or herd, or *whatever,* and keep their people in order.

So why wasn't Darius doing that?

It was a pretty hefty responsibility to abandon.

Was it all because of losing his wings?

I shook my head. Now wasn't the time to dwell on it. I'd grill him later when he couldn't steer the conversation elsewhere, or pretend to be *so* interested in what our two meathead security escorts were saying.

Because apparently, we were on the move—and I'd been so caught up in my thoughts that I hadn't noticed. Scampering after the trio, I gripped my backpack straps tighter and tried to keep up, all the while wondering what other secrets my dragon was hiding.

❧  9  ☙

WHEN RAVENA initially told us to head northwest to find a magical village named Aerath, I wasn't sure what to expect, honestly. As Darius and I had stomped through the woods, I'd started to envision wood huts in shambles. Tarps. Animal skins. It'd be like stepping back in time to something totally absurd. After all, if you wanted to live in a community of magic-inclined folks, it was just easier to create a settlement in Alfheim. At least there, you could practice your magic without restriction, free from the curious eyes of humans, and the limitations they wrought. So, to avoid detection, I'd just assumed the residents of Aerath would make the place look as decrepit as possible to encourage outsiders to keep on moving.

You know. A shanty town where it looked like you'd be stabbed within thirty seconds of arrival. That kind of thing. Much to my surprise, that wasn't the case. Not even a little. Sure, it still felt like we had gone back in time, but rather than going *all* the way back to the stone age, we were in a twentieth century English village in the countryside. Thatched rooftops. Stone walls—the kind that looked like someone placed each individual stone thoughtfully, and carefully. Cobblestone streets lay underfoot with gorgeous flower baskets in windows, and pristine awnings hanging in front of the entryways to the few small shops.

I'd felt the magic as soon as we stepped out of the forest. It washed over us like a great rushing wave, and while Darius merely stumbled and glanced around, unaware of what had just touched him, I recognized it immediately. While Liam and Colton were around for added muscle, the village magic practitioners had encased *everything* in a protection ward. There were *many* kinds of wards. The ones we used for our fae sister gathering kept us invisible, blocking outsiders from hearing or seeing us. It was old fae magic, but fairly standard. This ward, on the other hand, didn't hide the village, per se. Instead, it rushed over us like a giant scanner. The caster could set the terms, but should the ward detect something within any new arrival that was not permissible, it had the ability to punt us back out.

In a quaint place like this, I figured creatures like Vampires, Demons, Gremlins, Trolls—you know, the underbelly of the supernatural community—were probably unwelcome. Fairies and shifters, meanwhile, passed through unhindered.

"This is..." I bit my lip, carefully considering my words. While beautiful, the streets were empty, though I caught the flutter of curtains as we passed by the various thatched cottages. Someone must have tipped the inhabitants off that we were coming. Apparently, they didn't get very many visitors. When I caught Darius glance back at me—and both bears half-turned heads—I cleared my throat and quickly said, "Charming."

"I'd go nuts in a place like this," Darius muttered back, which made me smile. "I mean, what do you do as a kid here? It looks like a senior citizen's paradise."

"I kind of get the feeling that mischief is more punishable when you live in a place surrounded by magic."

Kids couldn't get away with egging people's houses and spray-painting fences because all it would take was a quick spell and it'd be gone. My eyes swept over the pristine white window shutters, most still open, and sighed. Darius was right. Any kind in their right mind would go a little deranged here—unless we weren't seeing the whole picture.

And with an almost *too* perfect exterior, I had to wonder what was lurking behind the scenes. Places that try too hard to appear flawless, usually have something to hide.

"You'll find Noris in there," Colton told us, gesturing with a nod of his head toward a cute little house on the top of a small hill. It had the greenest thatched roof—*was that grass growing on top?*—and a dark brown picket fence with flower baskets hanging, evenly spaced, around the whole thing.

Just as we started walking up the path, a perfectly manicured lawn on either side of the rustic cobblestone walkway, the door swung open and a hobbled man in what looked like Christian monk's garb stepped out. He blinked in the sunlight, thick glasses magnifying the fluttering of his eyes, then waved us forward with a frown.

"Well, come on then," he barked. "No need to dawdle. Business to attend to." He peered around us as both Darius and I picked up our pace. "Thank you, boys, that'll be all."

Colton and Liam waved goodbye to Darius before heading back toward the woods.

"You must be Darius," Noris remarked, appraising both of us with a hand shielding his eyes from the sun, "and you Kaye."

"Noris?" Darius held out a hand for the frail older mage to shake, which he did with some hesitancy. I bit my lip, trying not to laugh. If Darius pressed hard enough, half his regular strength probably, he'd snap those long, slender fingers right in two.

"The one and only," the mage said with a cackle once Darius released him. "Come along. Ravena said you'd be here yesterday. You're late."

We exchanged wary looks before following the hunched mage inside. The door closed on its own once we passed the threshold, and much to my embarrassment, I jumped a little at the loud thud it made.

While the village had been picturesque and postcard worthy,

Noris's home stunk of incense, and the air was thick with smoke. But not smoke from cooking, or a fire. As I blinked hard and held a hand up under my nose, I noted that the smoke reflected different shades when it was caught in the sun, like a rainbow had filled the open concept kitchen/living room area. Old hardwood creaked beneath our feet as Noris told us to follow him, and the stench of potion work and old charms only grew more potent as we descended what appeared to be a dirt stairwell into a workshop in the basement.

The mages I knew kept cleaner, less oppressive homes. Darius glanced back at me, face twisting from horror to disgust, to neutral in two seconds flat, and once again I had to hold back a giggle.

"How did Ravena tell you we'd be coming?" Darius asked. Noris seemed to have forgotten we were even there; he'd scuttled ahead and busied himself at a thick wooden table littered with half-melted candles, textbooks, and incense ash. "As far as I recall, she shuns most technology."

"There are more ways to communicate than with your hand-held electronics," Noris admonished, flipping one of those huge textbooks open and running a finger down a page. "She told me you are being hunted by Abramelin."

"*I* am," I said, shouldering my way in front of Darius before he could stop me. "He apparently sent a gargoyle to my apartment with an order to kill me, but I've never met him before. I don't know why he's after me, but Ravena says he's powerful."

"*Very*," Noris said, like it was the most obvious thing in the universe. "If he's after you, my first suggestion is to *run* and hide, my dear. Run and hide as quickly as you can. If Abramelin is after you, you're as good as dead."

I pursed my lips, trying not to stare at the shiny surface of his bald, age-speckled head. I couldn't ignore the fact that my heart was beating wildly in my chest, and for a minute I felt like I may get sick from my stomach turning at the thought of being chased down by a maniac. Then I remembered... I'm *not* some pathetically weak opponent, and I wasn't going to roll over and give up. Not for this fucking Warlock, not for anyone. "Yeah, that's not happening. I refuse to live my life on the run just because some asshole—"

"That *asshole* could crush you with a snap of his fingers," Noris told me, though his tone suggested the statement was more matter-of-fact than anything. "He's been on a rampage lately. Magical villages across the east coast have come under fire by him and his *goons*." Noris sniffed distastefully and straightened, though the movement seemed to pain him slightly. "Many in the magical community are fleeing to Alfheim for sanctuary. I suggest you do the same."

"So was I just caught in the crosshairs of some supernatural rampage by a psychopath?" I asked, hazarding a look back at Darius. The shifter stood in an uncharacteristically stoic silence, his jaw clenched and eyes fixed on Noris's grimoire. I shook my head and returned my gaze to Noris, frowning. "Why?"

"People seem to think I have inside knowledge of Abramelin's mind just because I trained him." Noris flipped rather dramatically to another section of his mammoth book, skimming the words for a moment, mouth moving rapidly as he read. *Speed reading.* Probably photographic memory. So, he truly was a very powerful mage. The guy didn't look like much, but he was probably the ace in the hole you'd want if you were ever backed into a corner. He glanced up with another sniff, then continued, as if the pause hadn't happened. "Abramelin was once good and just. In his youth, he was curious and capable, a prized student. The best I could have asked for. But..."

I watched his eyes grow distant as he stared right through me, and I cleared my throat. "But?"

"There are rumors," Noris said slowly, carefully, "that Abramelin's family was killed. Butchered, if I'm to believe the gossip. Since then, he's gone dark. Dangerous. Mad, possibly, as anyone might, under such horrible circumstances."

Losing your family didn't give you the right to go on a

murderous killing spree across innocent magical communities. I slid on my clinical hat once more, refusing to let my emotions get the better of me.

"Aerath is emptying," Noris muttered. When he looked up for a moment, his glasses slid back up his nose, magnifying his eyes. "The village will be gone in a week, or two. You are welcome to join us in Alfheim."

"We aren't going to run," Darius said gruffly, and I felt a distinct tightness in my chest at the sound of him agreeing with me. It was good to know we were on the same page. Over the last couple of days, we'd kind of become something of a team— yet now that other players were entering the game, I could only hope that bond would last.

"I cannot tell you how to defeat him," Noris told us, then raised a hand when, right on cue, both Darius and I started to protest. After all, the man was clearly powerful in his own right. I'd felt his magical aura before we even entered his cluttered, smoky, musty house. Noris fixed us with a rather impressive stare for a man his age, pointing hard to something within his huge grimoire. "*But...* I can cast a potent protection spell to keep you safe while you engage in this foolhardy quest to stop him." He turned his stare to me. "And it *is* foolhardy, but I sense stubbornness in you, fae and shifter alike. I am too old to fight stubborn fools in my own house."

Darius and I exchanged brief looks before Darius cleared his throat. "Thanks, I guess—"

"I'll need you to gather these items," Noris insisted, turning the grimoire around and pointing to a list written in tiny, neat scrawl. "It will not protect you from Abramelin himself. He is far too powerful. But it will keep his army at bay, and it will protect you while you make your way to Alfheim's portal." I held in a pointed sigh. No way we were running, but out of the corner of my eye, I noted Darius's head bobbing up and down. Apparently, he had other plans in mind. Noris snapped his fingers at us, then set us to work with a shooing motion. "Hurry now. It is a spell best cast when the sun is at its peak."

While Noris's list wasn't long, it took Darius and I quite some time to sift through all the crap piled up around his workshop. I hadn't ever sneezed so much in my life as I did digging through cobwebs and mountains of dust, but if the spell worked, it would all be worth it.

As per his instructions, we scrounged up three white candles, sage incense, and then added our signatures to a piece of parchment paper. We were both ordered to stand in the middle of the triangle formation Noris had made with the candles. As soon as we both stepped in, the wicks ignited on their own accord, their flames at least a foot tall at first before simmering down. I shuffled close to Darius, in no mood to be lit on fire in some old coot's basement.

"So, what's the deal here?" Darius crossed his arms, clearly unimpressed with the mage's somewhat archaic spellcasting. I nudged him and held a finger to my lips, to which he sighed pointedly and shut up. Noris, meanwhile, seemed not to notice the shifter's impatience. He used the candle at the point of the triangle to light his incense, then, much to my surprise—and mild horror—he tucked the incense stick behind his ear, burning end wafting a potent sage scent in our direction.

"I call upon the spirits of this realm and the next," Noris stated, his voice clear and firm, lacking the effects of age suddenly, "to protect Kaye and Darius from their enemies. May the spirits surround them and guide them until they cross through the Alfheim portal. May they live to see tomorrow's sunrise."

"Fantastic," Darius grumbled. I elbowed him a little harder this time.

Noris leaned down and ignited the parchment piece with our signatures on it with the nearest candle. He then let it drop into the triangular configuration with us, and as soon as the paper disappeared, consumed by flame, a rush of air slammed into us from all sides. I gasped; it was like experiencing a surge of powerful white magic. It was... beautiful, really. Uplifting. A sense of calm washed over me as I embraced the effects of the spell wholeheartedly. Using candles and incense and fire magic might have been old school, but Noris had just proved it *worked*.

Darius stumbled into me under the force of the spell, but we both managed to keep the other upright until the winds died down the moment the candlelight extinguished.

"There." Noris clapped his hands together like he was dusting them off. "Protected. And I know," he spoke over me when I drew a breath, as if sensing what I was about to say, "that you don't want to run. I still think you should go to Alfheim."

I made a face. "And hide?"

"And seek out a powerful fae there who can probably be more helpful than I've been," Noris told me somewhat pointedly, clearly sick of my attitude. "The supernatural community call him by the name of Z. He appears to be gathering an army of supernaturals with the express purpose of challenging Abramelin's power."

"Like a resistance?" Darius asked, though Noris quickly shook his head.

"Resistance implies Abramelin is the ruling party. I would call it more of a militia. A much-needed militia, who can stand up to a rather ruthless, and powerful bully."

"A *murderous* bully," I muttered under my breath. I felt a little light-headed when I stepped out of the triangle, a hand clutching Darius's arm to keep my balance. I did the same when he followed me a few seconds later. Once the feeling dissipated, I racked my memory for any mention of a powerful male fae in Alfheim who could do something like this, but quickly drew a blank.

But then again, if he was rallying fighters against Abramelin, a man who has literally been wiping out magical villages, I suppose you'd want to keep that quiet. No sense in alerting the enemy to your presence before you had the numbers to put up a proper fight.

"So now we have to go find a fairy named Z?" Darius asked, sounding just as skeptical of the whole thing as the rational side of me felt. I planted a hand on my hip to back him up, peering at Noris through the dimly lit workshop.

"And what's to say this Abramelin guy won't just enter Alfheim, root out this supposed army forming against him, and then wipe them out? If we all come together, we risk becoming sitting ducks."

"Magic is strong together," Noris said. "Fairies, witches, mages, elves, nymphs... even shifters—"

"Thanks for being inclusive," Darius grumbled, but Noris seemed not to hear him, as he prattled on.

"—stand a chance when they combine their power, their gifts. No chinks in the armor. No holes in the metaphorical shield wall, sort of speak." I pressed my lips together, not wanting to outwardly agree, but knowing the mage was right. *Strength in numbers.* Clearly Darius and I weren't strong enough to take on Abramelin by ourselves, and based on all that Noris had said, the guy didn't seem like he'd give up on something until it was dead, if he was as crazy as the rumors suggested.

"It really is our only option," Noris said, more to himself than to us.

I sighed. Apparently, we were running—to Alfheim.

## ❦ 10 ❦

ALFHEIM HAD many portals spread throughout the globe. The United States had one, or two, in every State, which ought to say something about the size of the supernatural community. However, the current data indicated that humans still outnumbered us by about half, so you always had to be on your guard not to let any human eyes catch you using one of those portals.

The portal closest to us was at a train station back in New York. So, after a somewhat awkward lunch with Noris, we were back on the road. I hadn't wanted to touch a single piece of food that came out of his dusty old kitchen, but I'd also been raised with manners, and refusing to dine at a man's table was a mortal sin in *many* communities. So, I ate. And I still felt the urge to gag every so often on the road when the memory of the dead spider I'd picked out of my sandwich flashed across my mind. A shiver ran down my spine, recalling the crunch and surge of foul taste in my mouth. It had been a freaking huge spider, hairy and plump, its blood staining my whole wheat.

"Still thinking about your extra protein at lunch?"

"Shut up," I grunted, shooting Darius a look that only made his smirk expand into a full-blown grin. As much as I hated to do it, I let him tease and have his laughs at my expense. Normally I wasn't so generous, but my dragon had been on edge about crossing the portal to Alfheim for the last hour of our drive. He wouldn't admit it, of course. Darius struck me as a man who refused to let *anyone* see his weaknesses; obviously, given his refusal to tell his family about his wing situation *and* the fact that he had abandoned his alpha duties—maybe, I had yet to confirm —because of it.

When it came to Alfheim, shifters were on the lower rung of a society that professed *not* to be a ladder. While there were a few shifter clans that called the realm their home, many preferred to live topside with the humans, rather than face the prejudices of the supernatural community. I couldn't blame him for being on edge, and as we pulled into the train station parking lot, I decided to use the other distraction I had up my sleeve, one that wasn't just poking fun at my mishaps.

I ran my fingers through my hair and cast a wary look to the train platform, which appeared empty for now. "Let's get this over with."

The portal was actually *under* the platform. There was a service door that came up to my waist and required a drop of supernatural blood to open. Darius's, unfortunately, wouldn't cut it. There were more than a few bigoted portal doors, and I knew some fairy friends who protested that fact around council buildings in Alfheim.

Although I just wanted to get the gargoyle fighting part over with, Darius forced us to sit in the parking lot for about twenty minutes while I recovered from gifting him with temporary foresight. Once I felt like myself again, we parked the car under the shade of some maple trees near the edge of the parking lot, next to the dumpsters. I then cast a quick bout of invisibility over us and my faithful vehicular transport; the spell, fueled by a surge of white magic, paired with an incantation for hidden objects in an old fairy language that I didn't understand, would cloak Darius, myself, and the car from human eyes, but it left us vulnerable to supernaturals. Most were encouraged to cast something similar when entering a portal to Alfheim, no matter the location, but there were some supernatural beings who were less preoccupied with the rules of our society, and more dedicated to where they needed to get to *now*.

A bit like my Manhattanites, honestly.

Bags and gear in hand, we crossed the parking lot, empty, save for two cars, then passed the gate and climbed the few stairs that led us up to the train platform. All was quiet, except for the rustling of the breeze through the trees, and the distant rumble of the nearby town's early evening traffic.

"Kaye—"

A roar filled the air, one that rattled the wood platform beneath our feet and sent a few candy bars tumbling from their shelves in the nearby vending machines. Darius and I whirled around, my dragon dropping his bags, and our eyes widened at the sight of gargoyles swarming up from above.

"They must have been in the trees," I grumbled, tossing my stuff aside and lifting to the balls of my feet, ready to call on fae speed to avoid the onslaught. There were so many of the damn creatures. Ten, by my count.

I raised my fists like I was ready for the fight of my life.

*Fuck.*

"Don't engage them unless you have to," Darius shouted to me over the battle cries of ten obnoxious gargoyles, their wings pounding the air with each stroke, sending up gravel and leaves in the parking lot as they crossed over. I looked at him, but he was already off, sprinting for the little metal roof over the trio of benches. My jaw dropped as he leaped onto it—the roof, not the benches—like he was hopping up a few measly stairs, and then it happened: Darius shifted.

Although he couldn't fly, Darius threw himself into the air, using the tin roof for footing, and shifted midair. One moment he was a man, a muscular *gorgeous* man, and the next he was a glorious dragon. His figure elongated—and just kept going, and going. He was red and orange, like the most stunning setting sun, neither color more prominent than the other. His scales rippled along with his movements, so agile and graceful for a creature his size. I couldn't help myself. My arms fell to my side, limp, as I full on open mouth stared at him in awe.

I'd never seen anything more beautiful in my life. And I had no issues referring to a very masculine, muscular dragon as beautiful—because that's *exactly* what he was. The size of a city bus, he slammed into the oncoming gargoyles and dragged them to the ground, probably crushing the few cars that were in the lot in the process, if the crunch of metal and muted car alarms were anything to go by.

When he disappeared from view—though definitely not from earshot—I realized my eyes had filled with tears. I blinked them away hastily, wiping a finger under each eye to catch the few that had fallen. Why was I feeling like this? Sure, Darius's dragon form was exquisite in every sense, but I didn't need to be...*emotional*. A tight fist locked around my chest, and my lips couldn't figure out whether they wanted to twist into a beaming smile or quiver with emotion. With want. With need. With... I shook my head and blinked hard, fists up again as two gargoyles plummeted toward me with all the precision of a runaway tanker truck.

While all I wanted to do was gawk at Darius's dragon, I knew I had to run, to fight. Still, my thoughts were set solely on him in that moment, gargoyles and all.

*Red*! I hadn't expected red. Maybe blue or dark green. But red was so vibrant and warm. Inviting. I suddenly yearned to trail my hands across his scales, across the black spikes running down the nape of his neck and fanning around his enormous face. Would they prick my finger if I touched them? They certainly looked sharp.

Thankfully, Noris's protection charm spared me from the first two blows, but the gargoyles refused to let up; they were programmed for destruction, and I couldn't let them stand. Darius had eight of his own to fight, so I dodged the next two hits, knowing the few that landed would have fractured bones had it not been for Noris's spell, and firmly told myself to put Darius out of my mind for now.

*Who would have thought a dragon could be such a distraction?*

Using my fae speed, I ducked and rolled, managing to get out from between the two snarling gargoyles. They followed faster than I'd expected, grabbing at my hair's tight ponytail and yanking me back. I felt a tingle of pain—a fraction of what it would be otherwise—and used the momentum against them. Jumping up, I twisted in the air and scaled the nearest gargoyle before he had a chance to grab me and slam me into the cement platform.

In the distance, I heard the distinct cry of a train horn. Knowing I'd never beat them on my own, and unsure if I could hold them off without Darius's help, a plan formulated—and fast.

"Hey, hey!" I shouted, clapping my hands and snapping my fingers as I jogged backward to the far end of the platform. The pair lurched after me, sickly yellow eyes blazing, and I knew I had them. It was a game of cat and mouse until the train was in sight, with me ducking and weaving and diving out of the way. My legs burned, displeased with all the fae speed I inflicted upon them, but I pushed on, knowing the timing was critical. The train didn't seem to be losing speed. It wasn't making a stop here.

*Perfect.*

I zipped to the edge of the platform, then braced myself for impact. As soon as the nearest gargoyle was within reach, I body checked him as hard as I could, throwing my elbow in firmly for good measure. The force managed to make him lose his footing and careen back into the gargoyle behind him. I then darted around both, pushing my fae speed to the limit so that I was just a blur to even the supernatural eye, then shoved both unstable gargoyles toward the train tracks. I threw in a pulse of white magic, just to be sure I had enough force behind me, and my careful timing paid off. Both gargoyles tumbled onto the track just as the train whizzed by. There was a crash, and I turned away, eyes closed, as the dust of broken gargoyles flew back at me, little bits of rock scratching my face like claws.

The train raced on, the cars rattling over the tracks, in just a few seconds. It gave one final blast of the horn to signify it was leaving town—and maybe as a warning from the conductor that any other gargoyles would meet the same grisly fate. Coughing, I moved to the edge of the platform. Sure enough, my attackers were gone, nothing but gray dust on the tracks.

Behind me, Darius's rumble shook the station, and as I whirled around, ready to join him, I suddenly felt a little woozy.

"Whoa..." I held a hand out to steady myself as I stumbled forward, catching my balance on the edge of a vending machine. My head hurt. My body hurt. *Everything* hurt.

Everything shouldn't hurt.

I touched a finger to my cheek and pulled away sharply as a warm wetness touched back.

Blood. I swiped again, just to be sure.

Yup, definitely blood.

Noris's spell must have been fading. He'd said it was only a temporary measure, but he could have allotted us a little wiggle room if we didn't make it to the Alfheim portal before nightfall. Shaking my head, I wiped the blood off on my clothes and took off running. If I was starting to feel the effects of the battle, I couldn't imagine how Darius was managing with *eight* gargoyles on his heels.

Well, make that four, apparently. As I surged down the steps and flung the gate open, I noticed piles of ashen attackers scattered across the lot. Sure enough, the poor cars had been crushed—though my baby remained safe far from the conflict. The gargoyles must have figured out that Darius couldn't fly; they attacked from above, dive-bombing him in the way crows do when you accidentally wander near their nest.

He managed to bite one out of the air, crushing it with his

jaws, but one landed and struck, stabbing a gleaming metal sword into Darius's side. My hands flew to my ears as the dragon cried out, a sound oozing both agony and fury.

"Fight fair!" I shouted, though I knew how silly that sounded. Still, neither of us had weapons. Where was the honor in *cheating*? Unable to watch from the sidelines a second longer, I rushed forward—only to get swept aside by Darius's massive tail. It knocked me clean off my feet, straight back into the gate. My head collided with the metal, and I won't lie; it fucking hurt.

"I'm trying to help, you stubborn bastard!" I snapped, knowing his sensitive little ears would hear me. Even if he did, he gave no hint of it: Darius managed to shake the gargoyle on his back loose. Then, once it was back in the air, he let all fiery hell break loose—literally.

They say the bluer the fire, the hotter the flame. While Darius's scales were both the setting sun and the crackling tip of a toasty bonfire in equal measures, the flame he breathed was pure blue. Even at a distance, the heat warmed my skin, and I rolled in on myself on the off-chance that any accidentally came my way. But the fire wasn't meant for me. It was meant for barbecuing the gnats hovering around my dragon's head—and barbecue them he did. All three were incinerated within seconds, showering the parking lot with black soot when the fire disappeared.

I looked up, eyes wide, when the heat died down and the crackle of flames, paired with a guttural growl emanating deep within Darius's chest, disappeared. My stunned silence lasted a few seconds before my will to survive—for both of us—kicked into play. I jumped to my feet and raced toward him as Darius's huge dragon head drooped forward, breathing hard and heavy through his flared nostrils. The first thing I did was yank the sword out, which caused him to growl, his lip curled up in a snarl.

I shrieked and tossed the sword aside when a burning pain

shot through my hands: iron. The damn thing was made of pure iron.

The bastard commanding those gargoyles certainly knew who he was going after. The sword landed with a clatter a few feet away, and there I'd leave it until Darius could touch it. Behind me, there was a rush of air, paired with what I could only describe as the crackling of bones. Gone was the enormous dragon, and in his place, a very naked Darius. He sat hunched on the ground, blood dripping from his side.

"Oh my god," I muttered, hurrying forward to inspect the wound. He tried to push me away, but I held firm. "How badly does it hurt?"

"S'fine," he insisted before pushing at me again. "Really. It'll heal."

"Not fast enough."

"Kaye." He let out a long, weary sigh. "Can you just get my clothes please?"

Heat crept up my cheeks as I finally processed the fact that he was buck naked. Huddling in on himself, however, I couldn't see anything...intimate. Nor should I be focusing on that. The stab wound on his side wasn't his only injury.

Stubborn as ever, he kept shoving me back when I tried to inspect the bloody marks across his body, so I raced back to the platform for our stuff, slamming the gate behind me for good measure, and was back by his side with his pack seconds later. I dug out an outfit, which he took with a little half smile, not quite as apologetic as I wanted.

"You're hurt badly," I stated, as he tugged the shirt on over his head. Biting my lip for a moment, I turned away to give him some privacy while he pulled the pants on.

"Like I said; I'll be fine," he said gruffly, and I whirled around with a scowl.

"Why are you always so stubborn?"

"It's not *that* bad," Darius argued, but as I let him struggle to his feet on his own, I crossed my arms and offered a cold laugh.

"You can barely stand."

"Work your magic then," he told me, his voice getting weaker by the moment. "Come on. Can you just do the healing stuff already, and we can get on with it?"

I threw my hands up in the air with a scoff. Fairies were skilled in many areas, and the use of medicinal herbs was one of them. I usually applied that toward the teas I gave my clients, knowing a specific tea would help with nerves, anxiety, and panic attacks. When my brother and I had been kids, we had a whole medicine cabinet of healing herbs, blessed by white magic because we were constantly skinning knees and breaking toes and getting ourselves into trouble in the woods near my aunt's house.

"I don't have any supplies," I snapped. Finally, he allowed me a moment to study the wound. When it continued to weep blood, I grabbed another pair of pants from his bag and used them to wrap the wound. It wasn't a permanent solution, but it might slow his blood loss for now. When I was through, I straightened up, hands on my hips, and fought the panicky prickle starting to grow in my core. This *was* a serious injury—one that needed immediate treatment. "We'll need to go to Alfheim immediately. The portal will take us to the city or to the woods, and I know I'll be able to find all I need in the forest."

After a blood payment was collected at the door, you had to choose 1 or 2 on a push-pad. Number 1: Alfheim city core. Number 2: the woodlands surrounding the main settlements. While I could rush Darius to a friend in the city, I knew it wouldn't be his first choice, and given how hardheaded he'd already been about me assessing him, I needed to go with what was easiest.

"Kaye, I still don't..." I dusted my hands on my pants as he trailed off, and when I glanced at him, I saw what he wouldn't want me to see. I saw the nerves. I saw the anxiety. I saw the panic.

Too bad I didn't have one of my herbal teas now.

"It'll be okay," I offered as gently as I could. "I know the shifter community isn't always well received in Alfheim, but we're together. We'll be fine."

"That's a lot of confidence there," he said with a weak chuckle. My eyebrows shot up.

I scooped up his bag on my way to brace him, sidling against his side and forcing him to use me as a crutch. He winced when we touched. That wound needed to be tended to—*now*.

"Look, we can either go to Alfheim," I said, knowing how to get him to stop protesting, "or we can go to your clan. They would probably have a better grasp on dealing with wounds of this nature—"

"Alfheim," he muttered gruffly, half-pulling me along beside him, half-leaning on me, as he steered us toward the train platform again. "We'll go to Alfheim."

I rolled my eyes. Now that I knew just a little more about him, manipulating him came easier.

And I wasn't sure if I was okay with that.

I needed to know about his past, his clan. I needed to know if he had a responsibility to *them*, something he was using me as an excuse to avoid in the meantime.

But for now, we just needed to get to Alfheim.

"It was a pretty selfless thing you did there," I noted as we took the steps one slow stair at a time. When he frowned at me, I added, "You know... Charging into a fight. It was... brave."

He shrugged with another wince. "I guess."

"Hey..." I stopped suddenly, the jerky motion making Darius grit his teeth. "Shouldn't you have your wings back then? You thought about someone else before yourself. You were selfless. Shouldn't that break the curse?"

"You'd think so," he grumbled, features hardening as he thought it over, "but I still couldn't fly during the fight. I think I'm still cursed."

*Not for long, hopefully*. He deserved something better than clipped wings. Shaking my head, I trudged on, his weight growing heavier and heavier as we approached the door. Just as I made my blood payment—a prick of my finger on a pristine silver nail sticking out of the door—the whistle of an oncoming train assaulted us, thunderous and shrill.

We were gone before it reached the station, tumbling between worlds.

Rushing, I hoped, toward salvation.

Not annihilation.

$$\approx \quad \text{I I} \quad \approx$$

FOR THE FIRST time in the history of our relationship, I woke up to find Darius still asleep. We had been in Alfheim for almost a week—roughly four days in the human world, as time moved differently here—and I had decided enough was enough on day one. I was fed up with this whole overbearing protector thing – it just had to stop. Darius wasn't standing guard over me while I slept anymore. It wasn't going to be a *thing*. I could take care of my damn self, and it was about time he acknowledged that.

First, however, we had had to deal with the gaping wound on the side of his (very-muscular) torso. We had crossed the portal between worlds together, which was always a dizzying, disorienting experience, no matter how many times I made that journey.

Humans classified the bridges between worlds in Norse mythology as the Rainbow Bridge, but I'd always had a sneaking suspicion that they created the myth because they somehow caught wind of the portals between Earth, and Alfheim. Like walking through a long, winding hallway, bright lights and swirling galaxies surrounded you as you crossed over. Below, your feet seemed to walk on air, as though you were fluid, weightless.

I'd always feared I would fall straight down into the darkness below, but it hadn't ever happened and I knew it was all in my mind. It would be a safe passage, as always.

The journey hadn't been as easy as it normally was, though, what with me balancing a hobbling dragon shifter on my body who weighed a freaking ton. It took *much* longer than expected, but eventually, we entered the woodlands, a good clip from the city center, and near the elvish settlements. There were scattered clans of orcs, goblins, and trolls in the forests too; creatures that the elves had been tasked with managing—when they weren't distracted by a pretty flower, or something equally absurd. I used to envy the elf way of life, carefree, for the most part, caught up in their daydreams and fantasies, far away from the realities of what the rest of us supernaturals had to deal with.

"Just stay here, and try not to bleed out," I had ordered once we found our bearings, gently depositing Darius at the base of an oak tree at the forest's edge. He'd smirked at my comment, shaking his head at my barking out orders. Obviously, he wasn't used to being told what to do by anyone, much less a fae, but I didn't care. He could growl all he wanted to, so long as he *actually* listened to me. Thankfully, this time he resisted arguing and remained seated on the forest floor while I surveyed the area, finding an elf cottage a few hundred yards away.

I'd then ventured inside, gathering what herbs I needed to make a suitable healing poultice. Thankfully, when I had returned with an armful of herbs and moss, Darius's accelerated healing powers had already kicked in, ensuring I didn't come back to find him bloodless and cold. After doing what I could to treat the wound, we started the long walk to the city center.

While Alfheim itself had many magical communities, supernaturals of all kinds clustered together in what was called the Core. Our council of elders gathered there, and most of our amenities were found there. Supernaturals without a clan, coven, Order, *whatever* could find a home there, welcomed with open arms. Supernatural species, in general, tended to inhabit their stereotype if they chose not to live in the Core. Elves dwelled in the forests. Goblins and orcs and trolls lived in the shadows and under mountains, competing with dwarves for territory. Vampires had grand castles in the foothills, extras added to make them as sun-free as possible. Demons lived... Well, I never quite understood demons, and what they did with themselves when they weren't busy bartering for human souls. They were shadow dwellers, for sure, with a tendency to just spring up *exactly* where you didn't want them, at *exactly* the wrong time. Thankfully, we had the Order of Angels—an elite demon-slaying task force—to take care of those nasty soul-suckers, so we weren't bothered by them that often.

Most of the fae I knew lived in the Core as well, preferring the ability to rent or buy, one of the fairy specialized homes there, equipped with zero iron, bolstered with white magic, and surrounded by their community of supernaturals. Some lived in nature. A few bunked up with the elves. But most of the fae I knew had modern tastes. We weren't immortal. We loved nature more than anything, but we didn't want to live in a hollowed-out tree trunk.

It was to the Core that I took Darius our first day in Alfheim. My poultice held firm as we marched from the woodlands to the city center, and before too long we were making our way to Belladonna's penthouse apartment. She had always let me stay there while she traveled around the human world, and I was excited to get settled. It was always so comforting to have a place to call home while in Alfheim.

I'd never learned how Belladonna acquired the funds to live the lavish lifestyle that she did, but owning a penthouse in one of Alfheim's swankiest apartment complexes was nothing new for her. The apartment spanned the entire top floor of the building, most of it open and sprawling with its fancy uptown loft vibes. Boxed in by a huge balcony crawling with wild ivy, the four bedrooms, two bathroom apartment had more than enough space for Darius and me, especially when we were the only ones in there. No way did we need the dwarven-crafted granite countertops or the luxurious Jacuzzi in the master suite.

I mean. *Maybe* we'd need it one day.

On our first day in Alfheim, however, the only thing that truly mattered with our housing was safety.

The whole building was surrounded by a protection ward, something I suspected Belladonna had a hand in crafting, as it positively pulsed with fairy energy. There was a beefy security team at the door at all times—and who could blame them, given the mischievous nature of *many* of my supernatural brethren?

All visitors had to be frisked, then signed up and escorted up to the upper-level apartments. After my I.D had been approved upon arrival, I'd dragged a wounded, weary Darius upstairs to the penthouse, and after leaving him to heal in one of the guest bedrooms, I'd scattered Ravena's protection stones everywhere for a little-added security, then cast a few white magic-fueled security measures of my own, just to be safe.

THE FIRST DAY HAD BEEN A BLUR, WITH MY BEING SO FOCUSED on Darius that I'd barely had a second to take Alfheim in. It had been almost eight months since I'd last visited, and while the magical world seldom changed, I always liked to immerse myself in it as deeply as possible, once I returned.

Thankfully, Darius was completely healed by the following morning, and so I took him to the local markets where sellers hawked their wares—all magical, all dangerous, most a rip-off. We explored the city, me acting as tour guide, to show Darius that it wasn't quite as bad as he thought it would be. The Core was a mishmash of ancient and modern architecture, most altered magically by its inhabitants: houses shaped like a triangle, but sitting point-side down; hovering apartment blocks for the upper echelon who preferred no contact with us ruffians; man-eating plants reaching out for you from their oversized flower boxes; enchanted shop signs that shouted at you if you didn't pay them any attention.

The Core was a *lot* to take in—like Manhattan in many respects, but I didn't find the Core draining like I did New York City. All the different kinds of magic rejuvenated me. Alfheim's air was thick with it.

And I tried to fill my lungs with it as deeply as possible.

With each passing day, Darius had relaxed—but only slightly. His fears weren't unfounded. After all, Abramelin was undoubtedly still on the hunt for me after Darius fried his gargoyles, and while we did our best not to draw attention to ourselves, I just couldn't sit in the penthouse all day and try to research Z from a distance. We'd both known we had to get our hands dirty in the Core—be where the action was, as it were.

We both carried protection stones wherever we went and had purchased a few droughts from the witch apothecary around the corner from Belladonna's apartment. When consumed, the potions we chose would make us difficult to remember to all those we met in passing. They would know a fae and a shifter had just walked by, but our faces would never be clear.

Speaking of a shifter in Alfheim... We *did* get some odd looks from all sorts of creatures as we had strolled through the Core's main streets and side alleys. Supernaturals could sense you in a heartbeat. They all knew I was fae—and they all knew the company I kept. I'd kept my head held high, refusing to let their stares affect me, one way or another. It had been good for Darius to have my support, just as I had his while we'd searched for this mysterious fairy named Z.

A week of searching hadn't turned up much. Most of my contacts merely knew of the name, had heard rumors and whispers, but no one could point to *anything* definitively. Each day Darius and I asked around—discreetly, of course—and each day, we turned up nothing.

I couldn't imagine that today would be any different, but we would still make our rounds, and try to uncover this mysterious fae.

As I gently closed the door to the guest room where Darius slept, I made a mental list of other things to do: get breakfast from the market, take Darius exploring in the elvish village on the outskirts of the Core like I promised—and when we were there, press them for information about Z. There was a nymph-held production in the amphitheater near Belladonna's five-story apartment building this afternoon, which I thought would give us a nice opportunity to study the Core's inhabitants in a subtle way. Then dinner. Then stargazing on the wraparound balcony. Then... wherever the night took us.

After swapping my sleeping attire—which was nothing more than an oversized t-shirt that I left in the apartment for when I visited—for a golden yellow sundress, I slipped on my shoes and made my way to the street below. The doorman, a dryad with skin like bark and hair like moss, swept down in a low bow as he held the door open, to which I smiled awkwardly at.

The morning market was just a few blocks over. One might think the streets would be set in a logical pattern, but for the most part, the streets in the Core were like ivy branches: they went whatever way they damn well pleased, winding around each other, and back again. At least by now, I knew the streets by heart, and my feet didn't lead me astray. Hell, even if my eyes *were* closed, the sounds of the morning market chaos would be enough to guide me to the right place.

The market spanned two blocks and all the streets, nooks, crannies, and awnings within it. Sellers sold meat, grain, and handbags all in one area. There was no sense of cohesion, no logical, organized placement for different types of goods and services. The merchants simply set up their stands in the morning, just before dawn, and fought for the best spot each day.

I wove through the crowds, on the hunt for *very* particular sellers. A little gremlin—literally—cut me off at one point, darting in front of me and whipping open his trench coat like he was in a cheesy eighties movie.

"You wanna buy some angel feathers?" he demanded, wriggling his eyebrows at me as I stared on in horror. Fluffy white feathers lined his coat—some still with blood rooted to their base. He coughed, a smoker's hack if I'd ever heard one, and added, "Genuine feathers. Freshly plucked. Loaded with the ability to make you *soar*, baby girl."

"You're absolutely disgusting," I spat angrily, then purposefully strode around him, knocking roughly into his arm on the way by. I heard some incoherent grumbling behind me, then seconds later the same spiel was prattled off to another unsuspecting victim, and I found myself cringing, repulsed by it all.

Not all the sellers in the Core were as good as the guys I bought my breakfast supplies from.

All my food was iron free, purchased directly from fairies in the community. Bread. Eggs. Cheese. Bacon. Everything was Alfheim-grown and cured. As much as I'd wanted to ask about Z, a crowded market where anyone might be listening just wasn't the place. So, I forked over my silver coins—which I'd had converted from American dollars my second day here—and headed back to the apartment. Three silver coins amounted to roughly forty US dollars in the human world, something I always forgot about when I visited. It was so easy to just toss a coin here and there, especially when the price of goods looked so cheap. One silver coin for a pound of my *favorite* Kitchen Witch brand of cheese? Yes, *please*. I did it all the time, every visit, without fail. Alfheim just wound me up too much—and then I'd realize I'd dropped three or four hundred dollars in a day, and suddenly my spending budget was sliced in half.

That had happened on our second day when I bought Darius a hilarious Hawaiian-themed shirt and forced him to wear it, unable to help myself.

Twelve silver coins later, the purse strings tightened.

I arrived home, my arms filled with my bounty. Just as I was locking the front door, I heard Darius call my name from the bathroom over the sound of running water, obviously taking a shower. I called his name back, distracted by the mail that had been pushed through the door, sitting in a pile at my feet. All for Belladonna and her girls, of course. I snatched it up from the ground, filtering through the junk mail and envelopes, checking to see if there was anything important I should set aside for Belladonna, as she had requested of me the last time I was here. Much to my annoyance, one of the flyers decided to spontaneously combust when I tried to throw it away.

Apparently, if you weren't interested in being a customer of Witch's Brew Emporium, you deserved to have your eyebrows singed off.

Darius called my name again, and I set our breakfast goods down on the kitchen island with a huff. "*What*, Darius?"

"Come here!"

I bit my lower lip for a moment, then padded across the expansive apartment to the guest bathroom. It seemed unlikely he was about to ask me to join him since he was, you know, so focused on *duty* and what was appropriate for a "client". I was in the middle of a huge eye roll just thinking about it when his head popped out of the doorway—and, embarrassingly enough, I jumped and cried out in surprise.

"Damn it, Darius," I muttered as he laughed. "Did you call me over here just to scare me?"

"No." He motioned for me to step into the insanely humid bathroom. Dragons and their scalding hot showers. Seriously. Shower sex was getting less and less appealing the more I learned about him.

"So, what is it? I can go to a sauna with the ice elves if I wanted—"

"Did you write this?"

I frowned. "Write what?"

"The message." He stared at me hard for a moment. "On the mirror."

I blinked—it was like trying to see through sticky, invasive fog in here—and so I moved closer to look.

*I HEAR YOU'RE LOOKING FOR ME*

"Yeah, I definitely did *not* write that," I told him, trailing off as I studied the writing. It looked like a man's writing, honestly, lacking the loopy, fatness most women's writing had outside of the medical professions. "When did it appear?"

"It wasn't there before I got into the shower," he replied, shrugging. His voice had lost some of its joking edge, hints of concern now seeping through. Just as he was about to say something further, the writing vanished, and I gasped as more, new writing started to appear—like we were watching someone write it. I lashed out around the sink, trying to feel for a spirit or a disgusting invisible man who liked to hide in people's bathrooms —but sensed nothing. I then switched to my second sight, but beyond the colorful pulses of the standard magic one might find in a fairy's apartment in Alfheim—again, I found nothing.

"What the hell..." I squinted at the new message.

*FIND THE GRAVE MARKED WITH THE SUN*
*THERE WILL YOU FIND ME*
*- Z*

"Well, looks like he found *us*," I stammered, a rush of prickling anxiety coursing through me. "Z."

"Or it's a trap," Darius countered, and we exchanged a quick raised-brow look with one another. It could very well *be* a trap. Maybe someone caught wind that we were looking for a fairy rebel and wanted to stop us before we joined his ranks. Maybe Abramelin liked fucking with his prey before he killed it—which, given his past actions, would strike me as odd. Sending assassins to kill me, twice, was a pretty straightforward way of doing things.

"We aren't going to see the elves today," I said softly. When I reached out for the mirror, curious as to whether the lettering would feel like anything familiar, the words vanished and were quickly replaced.

*KAYE. HURRY.*

MY EYES WIDENED, ANXIETY SPIKING IN AN INSTANT. Z KNEW my name. He knew *me*.

"No," Darius remarked, totally oblivious to my internal freak-out at the name drop. "Apparently we're going to visit the dead instead." He paused as I gawked at my name, heart pounding. My dragon then gave a curt exhale, something that sounded like a cross between a groan and a growl. "Fantastic."

"YOU SEE ANYTHING YET?"

I blew a few recently fallen dark red locks out of my face, not wanting them to stick to my sweaty forehead. "Nope. You?"

"Not really, no."

I groaned softly, then brushed away the dirt and weeds from yet another gravestone. Nothing about the name indicated a sun, a relation to the sun, or even sunshine. I hadn't so much as seen a single *you're the light of my life* on any of these things. Most of the stones were just names, many in runes well outside my vocabulary, which only made things harder.

After breakfast, Darius and I had made our way to the Core's only graveyard. It was on the outskirts of the city, closer to the scarier magical forests than those full of elves and nymphs, and the like. Scary trees. Scary dark shadows. Scary noises and whispers I could have *sworn* sounded like my name. Just... scary overall.

The graveyard itself wasn't scary, and it shouldn't be, given the fact that we searched through it in broad daylight. Z hadn't given us anything else to work with besides the vague sun comment, so we initially thought that maybe some beam of sunlight would wash over a single tomb or grave marker.

Of course, it could never be that easy.

We'd been at it for two hours and hadn't seen a soul—living, or otherwise. Centuries worth of dead supernaturals lay beneath our feet. Those that didn't turn to ash or stone, or whatever when they died, ended up here, near their kin, if possible. And throughout our searching, I'd seen more fae runes on graves with young fairies buried beneath than I could have imagined.

The sun was unrelenting today, not a cloud in the sky, which made for hot and exhausting work. I was on the verge of calling it quits, with the plan to go grab some lunch and regroup, maybe contact Noris again to see if he had any suggestions, when something caught my eye. It happened in passing. I wasn't even looking at the headstone, but my brain processed the shape and stopped me in my tracks.

It was a headstone with no name, in the middle of a row of clan-less supernaturals. No name—but instead, a small sun insignia carved into the corner.

"Darius!" My voice echoed across the lot, and he hurried over, carefully making his way around the graves.

"What?" He looked just as sweaty as I did, which made me

feel a little better. I pointed to the carving, before wiping at my forehead.

"A sun."

His head bobbed up and down. "So it is. You think that's it?"

"Only one way to find out."

Touching it didn't seem to do anything. Both Darius and I tried to push, pull, and prod the carving into doing *something*. Each failure dampened my spirits just slightly, but it didn't extinguish them. This was the first sign of something meaningful we'd found all day. It *had* to be something; it just had to be.

"Wait." I managed to stop Darius from straight-up punting the gravestone across the row, noting the way his forehead crinkled in frustration. "Wait. Let me try something…"

Maybe this was another bigoted portal. Maybe it needed a supernatural blood sacrifice for us to cross through.

I pricked my finger on the sharp edge of the gravestone, then pressed my bloodied tip to the center of the sun. Seconds later, the ground under my feet started to rumble and vibrate, and Darius yanked me away, just as the earth disintegrated beneath me. Arms wrapped tight around my waist, he set me down behind him, then peered inside.

"Stairs," he said, and I darted around him. Sure enough, a set of stone stairs awaited us, a little dirty, but otherwise stable. Torches illuminated the way down, and I let out a shocked laugh.

"An underground world *in* an underground world," I said, sighing, and shook my head. "Un-fucking-believable."

"Let me go first," Darius insisted, and just as I started to protest, a figure stepped into the light at the bottom of the stairs, shutting us both up—but for different reasons, I suspected.

Because standing there, peering up at me, was a man who reminded me of my father.

But he wasn't my father.

He was my *brother*.

My heart seemed to split in half, flying up into my throat and plunging down into my stomach at the same time. It was hard to swallow, to think, to stand.

"Zayne?"

He grinned up at me, and maybe it was just a trick of the flickering torchlight, but I swore he looked just as he did the day he left me all those years ago. "Hey, sis…"

## 🦋 12 🦋

FOR A SPLIT SECOND, I felt like a little girl again. I threw caution
to the wind and flew down those stairs, barreling into Zayne so
hard that I sent him stumbling back. What hit me immediately
was that he smelled the same as I remembered. Smells are hard
to describe, but you are immediately transported to a memory
from your childhood when a familiar, nostalgic one hits you. It
creates that warm glow in your belly and forces a smile across
your lips, no matter your mood. Zayne's scent hit me right away,
hard, like a punch to the gut, and I held tight, breathing him in.

We had the same dark red hair, and he had let his grow
shaggy and wild down to his shoulders. In the history of the fae,
patriarchs and matriarchs tended to wear their hair wild, like the
bigger and rattier it was, the more power they'd absorbed from
the elements. I grasped the back of his head, that hair impene-
trable as we hugged, and I felt him do the same.

We both trembled in one another's arms, and when I finally
pulled back, despite every fiber of my being protesting the
distance, I noticed the tears in his eyes—they mirrored the ones
in mine. We both wiped them away, sniffling and grinning like
idiots, and in that moment, all my anger with him, all the
baggage he'd dumped on me when he left me all alone, was gone.

The psychologist in me knew it would rear its ugly head soon. It would *have* to be dealt with if we had any hope of moving forward, but for now, I just wanted to look at him, to hug him.

"Zayne..." I pressed a hand to his cheek. While mine had retained some baby fat well into my adult years, his had grown sharp and hard, cheekbones defined and lips thin, just like our dad. I blinked hard when sad memories began to surface, then cocked my head to one side. "Wait, are you... Are you this Z character?"

He nodded. "I am. I didn't want to involve you in any of this, but when I heard you were looking for me, I knew there had to be a reason."

"Oh, yeah, definitely a reason. Abramelin tried to kill me," I told him, noting the hardening look in his eye and the way his grip on my arm tightened. "I was told to find Z, that I couldn't take him on alone."

"No, you couldn't," my brother agreed. His voice had gone soft, contemplative, and behind me I heard Darius's slow, hesitant footsteps coming down the stairs. "It's good that you came to Alfheim."

"Is this... still Alfheim?" I asked, gesturing to the sprawling landscape around us. It was the first time I even processed where we were, and the only thing I could compare it to were the old paintings of dwarven halls from the ancient days. Modern dwarves still mined deep into the mountains, both in our supernatural world and the human world above, but no one had great halls like this anymore—the kind where you couldn't quite see the ceiling, and the great stone pillars glittered like diamonds in the torchlight. Over Zayne's shoulder, I spotted a handful of men and women waiting. I frowned. Did my brother have an entourage?

I probably shouldn't have been surprised. After all, my big brother, the guy who used to be frightened of the furnace in our aunt's basement, was leading an underground militia, hell bent on stopping a psychopathic ArchMage, and his minions.

*Why shouldn't he have an entourage?*

"Yes, we're still in Alfheim," he told me quickly, "but the door is sealed... It only opens for fae blood." When I tried to ask yet another of my thousand questions, all of them swirling around in my head like a hurricane, he gave me a little shake and dipped down to my eye level, frowning. "Kaye, I know you must have a million questions for me, and I promise I'll answer them all when the battle is over."

My eyebrows shot up. "The...battle?"

"It's coming," he insisted, eyes sparkling with a manic energy I'd never seen before. I swallowed hard, not liking what I saw, as he continued, "My sources are never wrong. We need to get you armed and ready. There's a whole host of new spells I can teach you to better defend yourself, but make no mistake, Abramelin *is* coming for us. We've been attacking his forces for months now. I think he considers us flies, buzzing around a larger predator, but I'd like to think we're a spider drawing *him* into our web."

I gawked, unsure of what to say. A part of me had known that once Darius and I found Z, we would probably have to fight in some way. After all, who would offer us sanctuary without expecting a little payment in return? This *was* an unofficial militia, after all. Still, I hadn't expected to be thrust into all of this so suddenly—*especially* after only just reconnecting with Zayne.

"We've been building up our numbers with supernaturals from all over the country," Zayne told me, finally appearing to calm himself. I couldn't blame him. Clearly, he was passionate about defeating a psychopath and keeping our world safe. It was just... It was an odd feeling to look at the man in front of me, a man I grew up with, and not really *know* him anymore, despite the familiar face and nostalgic scent.

"And you're all going to fight?"

"We are." He nodded, the fire still burning brightly behind his eyes. "Abramelin has become a public menace to the supernatural community. And it isn't just in the United States that people are pledging to fight. Supernaturals from all over the human world have joined our ranks. He must be stopped."

"I don't understand *why* Abramelin is attacking supernaturals, though," I said, arms crossed over myself, suddenly feeling too small in a big world. "I haven't... I didn't *do* anything to him."

"It's revenge," my brother remarked without missing a beat. "He returned home one day to find his family slaughtered... Literally ripped to shreds."

The knot in my stomach grew tighter, more painful. "But who would do that? Supernaturals don't..."

We don't rip people apart. Most supernatural beings have magic at their disposal if they want to destroy someone or something.

"It wasn't magic that did it," he told me, slowly, almost carefully, his gaze flicking over my shoulder in Darius's direction. "It was a clan of shifters."

"Shifters?" I shook my head. "But then why... Why go after supernaturals? Why go after *me*? I didn't *do* anything."

The look he gave me was pained for a fleeting moment, but not so fleeting that I missed it. But with a few rapid blinks of his emerald green eyes, it was gone, replaced by a steely hardness that unsettled me.

"He's going after anyone who sympathizes with shifters first," Zayne said, scowling. "Anyone who isn't a total bigot is on the chopping block. Anyone who would defend them, who would fight by their side are a target because together, supernaturals and shifters are a force to reckon with. Undefeatable. We're all dying because a clan of shifters—"

"Hey," Darius barked, making both my brother and me jump. "Shifters don't just slaughter a family for no good reason. We're not mindless beasts."

While I'd noticed Zayne glance back a few times during our conversation, it was as though this was the first time he had actually *seen* Darius—and his scowl didn't seem to be going anywhere anytime soon.

"Who is this?" he demanded, stepping to the side to appraise Darius without me being in the way. "Why is he here? He isn't *fae*—"

"Not on your life, pal," Darius growled before I could stop him.

Zayne gave the dragon one last quick up and down look before beckoning one of his entourage over.

"See that this *shifter* finds his way back to a portal—"

"No," I cried, hastily positioning myself between Darius and anyone who wanted to hurt him. "*No*. Darius is my friend. We made a deal that we would work together until I was no longer in danger. We're sworn."

Zayne's expression flashed from surprise, to incredulous, in a heartbeat. "You made a *deal* with this man? Kaye, you *know* how precious deals are to us. How could you?"

"Because I trust him," I said forcefully, my words wobbling with a bit of unexpected emotion. "He vowed to keep me safe. Where he goes, I go." My gaze darted to the entourage, two of whom had stopped awkwardly between the others and Darius, clearly unsure about what they were supposed to do. I raised my chin at them. "Darius stays."

When I looked at Zayne, I caught the brief flicker of his jaw —like he was clenching. Our dad used to do that. Finally, he sighed and motioned for his men to step back.

"As long as he stays in line," my brother insisted, "*and* he does his duty to keep you out of danger, then your friend has a place in this fight." His eyes honed in on Darius, possessing a strength I'd never known my brother to have. "Do *not* make me regret this."

"Yeah, whatever," I heard Darius mutter stiffly in return. A quick glance over my shoulder showed me he was clenching his fists. "I'll be a good dog, Z."

"A good *dragon*," I countered, squaring my shoulders. "Darius can fight. I've never seen a fire as blue as his. He is an asset and an ally. You should treat him as such."

While my brother seemed to be studying Darius with a newfound, perhaps temporary, sense of respect, Darius appeared to be doing the same—only with me, and not Zayne. I shifted my weight back and forth between each leg, uncomfortable with the dragon's unflinching gaze. Thankfully, Zayne was the one to break the silence.

"I wish I could stay longer, Kaye, but there are a million things to do down here," Zayne told me, sounding like a strange mix of Brother and Leader, but not settling hard on either in the moment. He took my hands in his and gave them a squeeze. "I've organized lodgings for you. Eilie will show you to them, and I'll have some of the others find space for your friend."

"But how did you know we were coming?" Darius asked, his brows furrowed.

Zayne chuckled, and looked from Darius to me with an expression that indicated he was clearly amused by the question. After all, he was a powerful fae. More powerful than I would ever hope to be. He was also the one that led us here.

"Magic, of course. And well, word carries quickly around Alfheim. You were looking for me, and I was looking for my sister."

Over his shoulder, a fairy woman—Eilie, I assumed—gave me a nod and a smile, though her cheeriness faltered somewhat when Darius stepped up to my side.

"I'll need to be close," Darius said. "I'm on duty twenty-four-seven when it comes to your sister."

"It will be done. Stand by her side. I'm sure you know how much she'll need you."

And then he was releasing my hands and stepping away from me—and it was like he was abandoning me all over again. I staggered forward and clutched at him. "Zayne..."

"Kaye, I know this is tough—"

"But why me?" I whispered, like a little girl lost to the world.

"Why would he try to kill me? I don't *do* anything with shifters, politically speaking, anyway. I just... exist."

There it was again, that pained expression. Gone just as fast as before, too.

"We'll talk about everything," he said softly, then pressed a hard kiss to my forehead. I closed my eyes, just for a few seconds, and let myself feel like that lost little girl—until he pulled away. "I promise, Kaye. You and I will talk until there are no more words left to say. Just...later."

I nodded slowly, resigned to my fate. "Okay."

He shot Darius one last look, of neither contempt nor acceptance—more curiosity than anything—before stalking back to his entourage. I watched them chat for a moment before Zayne strode from the huge hall, his footfalls like thunder in my ears.

His entourage split behind him, half following my brother out, while the others went in the opposite direction, toward an arched open doorway with old fae runes carved along the outside. Seeing as Eilie was among the group headed for the door, I assumed Darius and I were supposed to follow.

The strange thing was—I just couldn't make my feet move.

"Hey..." Darius's hand clamped down on my shoulder, harder than either of us expected, and I lifted my gaze to him.

"Hey."

"How you doing?" he asked as he crouched a little in front of me, our eyes meeting. "That was a lot at once." Then, under his breath, he added, "And not the way I would have done it."

"I don't know how I feel," I admitted. There were too many feelings to process about all the shit that had just gone down, and, honestly, I wasn't in the right frame of mind to even *try* and dissect them. But standing there with Darius, alone in a huge hall, safe from all our problems for just a few minutes, I felt an odd sense of peace washing over me. After all that, shockingly, I was just glad to have Darius with me.

"It's okay not to know how to feel about all this," he told me, and my cheeks warmed when he tucked my hair behind each ear.

"I know." With a soft clearing of my throat, I tried to smile, just to diffuse the situation, to break the focus away from me. "I'm the psychologist, remember? I just don't know what he meant about you knowing I'll need you, though. I'm pretty sure I don't need anyone. In fact, I'm pretty sure I'm the toughest motherfucking fa—"

My words were lost in the crush of his kiss, and while he silenced my mouth, my heart screamed wildly in my chest. I let out a shocked puff of air, his lips warm and firm against mine. Heat bloomed throughout my body, curling in my core, a wispy, feathered surge of unexpected pleasure.

We had kissed before, of course. We'd touched frequently since then. But something about the way he held me, the way his lips parted and his tongue slid between mine—it was electric. I could practically feel my hair rising, the crackle of static making me blush. Unsure of just about everything, my hand crept up to rest on his chest, as my eyes fluttered shut, losing myself in the moment. As his arm curled around my waist, my hand wandered up just a little more, cupping his cheek and caressing the stubble there with a sweep of my thumb. Our tongues brushed against one another, tentatively at first, but growing more insistent, more demanding, until finally, it wasn't just the curious caress of tongues, but also the occasional crashing of teeth, the kiss turning more desperate the longer he held me in his arms.

Could he hear my racing heart? Pounding hard and fast within my chest, I realized in that moment it beat solely for Darius as it never had before. Unable to stop myself, I moaned softly. Seconds later his fingertips bit down on my flesh, and I mourned the fact that we were still wearing *clothes*, and that those bruising fingers wouldn't leave pleasant little reminders across my hips for tomorrow morning...

Just as I was on the verge of yanking his T-shirt off and pouncing on the buckle of his black leather belt, Darius eased away—as per fucking usual, nothing out of the ordinary with my dragon. I tried to follow, to recapture what we had, but he kept me in place.

"I just had to stop that bullshit before you started to believe it," he whispered, breath hot on my face, his chuckle warming my heart. "You're not the toughest motherfucking fairy. You're a strong woman who shouldn't have to carry the weight of the world on her shoulders. Don't forget that. Ever. I'm here to share some of that burden of yours, whether you want me to, or not."

I lifted an eyebrow. "I don't really have a choice, do I?"

"No." Darius grinned as we slowly untangled our limbs. "You don't. We made a deal, remember?"

That we did. I was essentially stuck with Darius until Abramelin was dead and buried.

I did my best not to shy away from him, but the kiss had truly caught me off guard, and a thousand sensations still buzzed through my body, leaving my skin on fire, and my pulse racing. I suddenly wasn't sure how to act around him, or what my next move should be – only that I *desperately* wanted there to be a next move. However, when Darius didn't immediately follow me toward the door that Eilie had gone through, I turned back to face him, planting a hand on my hip.

"What's up? You waiting for a personal invitation, or something?"

His lips curved into a smile, and he chuckled, his eyes never moving from my face. "I'm going to go talk to your brother," he told me, and when I started to argue, he took a step back, still wearing that easy smile that made my knees weak. "I need to make sure that I won't run into any trouble because of my, well, heritage."

I frowned. No one was going to hassle Darius just because he was a shifter. Not here, at least. Not in an army that wanted to combat intolerant assholes. "Fairies keep their word, Darius."

"Yeah, well, not all do," he fired back, and Jasmine's smug, stupid face flashed across my mind. "I'll catch up. Go on. Make sure we get a room with a view."

I couldn't help but sigh as I watched him walk away, wishing he could have seen that I needed him to hold me up—just for a little while until the crumbling pieces of my reality melded back into place. But I was apparently going to have to do that on my own.

Which was fine. I'd been surviving heartache all by my lonesome for years now.

I could do it just a little while longer.

❧ 13 ❧

I AWOKE from a dead sleep feeling like I hadn't had a second of rest. Blinking heavy, I stared up into the blackness, temporarily forgetting that I wasn't waking up in my bedroom—or a motel, or a tent, or the back of my car. I was in Alfheim, deep underground, in a hidden sanctuary crafted by magic from all sorts of supernatural beings. It had been a little overwhelming at first. Once we left that huge hall with Eilie and the other fairies, it had been an ongoing assault of various kinds of spells, charms, hexes, and power. Just as my brother had said, there were beings from all races, all species, banded together in secret to fight the growing threat that *was* Abramelin.

Zayne's sanctuary was like a beehive—both literally and figuratively. In the literal sense, it seemed to cut down into the earth like a cone, with various levels for different deeds. You could lean over the railing and see straight down to the bottom level, from which grew a castle, its tallest tower nearly reaching the top floor. That was where I'd been offered a room. Dormitories for the others were on the sixth floor—of eight—and Zayne, along with his council of elders, holed up inside the castle.

In the figurative sense, the underground world within an underground world was much like a beehive in its insane amount of activity. People were always on the move, doing something, talking, laughing, shouting to one another. It was like the morning market on steroids, and it gave me both a sense of peace—it was fabulous to see so many different people rallying to fight a common enemy—and an insane headache. Because, it was all *very* chaotic. Organized chaos, sure, but it would probably take me a day or two to get used to things.

I ended up spending the whole day without either Darius or Zayne for company which didn't sit well with me. While the castle attendants were good about making sure I was eating enough, and giving me a tour of the facilities, I just wanted one of those two guys back by my side. I hadn't come to Alfheim to feel lonelier than I did sometimes in Manhattan—after a day of listening to difficult, traumatizing stories from clients, shouldering their burdens, and trying to help as best I could, sitting alone in my apartment in front of the television just didn't cut it. As I'd crawled into bed earlier that night, exhausted, I felt much the same way: drained, and very much alone.

*So much for pretending to be a tough, independent woman, right?*

Yet here I was, hours later, still tired as hell. I rolled over, burying my face in the soft, squishy pillow with a groan. Unfortunately, all my tossing and turning did nothing to help me feel better. Sleep remained elusive, and soon enough, I just threw the covers off and rolled out of bed.

The room Zayne had arranged for me was spacious and covered the entire top floor of the castle's tower. My new bed had to be just shy of king-sized, yet I noticed I'd only done my tossing about on one side. There were two couches, and a few bookshelves, plus some sinfully dated shag carpets. Someone had laced the room with protective draughts, and earlier, during my investigation of everything, I had found little charm pouches full of protective herbs and gemstones, all infused with white magic. I should have felt safe, like there was nowhere better to be in all the worlds.

But for some reason, despite all that, I couldn't sleep.

Sighing, I dug through my bag for a housecoat. The silken material could basically fold into nothing, so I'd stuffed it in there last minute before Darius and I left the city. Now I was pleased, as I was too tired to change into something more presentable. So, clad in my silky black housecoat and a tank-shorts combo, I headed for the balcony. A quick scan through the floor to ceiling glass doors told me Darius wasn't crouched on the railing, watching over me, and our surroundings. In fact, I couldn't feel him *anywhere* nearby, and the thought made my stomach twist.

Maybe he was on the roof? It seemed absurd, but I could totally picture Darius perched amidst the huge slate gray shingles, analyzing this new world in silence. So, I unlatched the series of locks that kept the windows closed, then slipped out onto the balcony. A gust of warm wind blew my robe wide open, and I hastily scrambled to get it shut, and tie it around my waist.

Not that I needed to hide from anyone. Darius wasn't on the tower's roof. My heart sunk just a little bit more than I would have liked, as I scanned the area. *Nothing.* Not a dragon for miles. Exhaling deeply, I turned and leaned against the balcony's stone railing. Thick and sturdy, it seemed like it could support a fairy who was dealing with some heavy personal bullshit.

Biting the inside of my cheek, my gaze traveled outward to take in the underground world around me. At least if I was studying architecture, I might not think about a certain dragon.

*Who'd kissed me out of nowhere.*

His lips leaving mine buzzed and warm, my stomach in knots, my lady parts all...

*Ha.*

Fat chance the landscape could distract me from my dragon.

Still, it was beautiful down here, even at night. The whole beehive thing had gone out the window, and while the shape hadn't changed, the energy certainly had. I could feel the pulse of magic, thick and present, just as it was above ground. Yet here my heart raced. Each breath was invigorating in a new sort of way like I was suddenly filled with hope.

Was it just the place? Was it the fact that all around me, supernaturals were gathering to defeat the jerk who had tried to put me six feet under? Or had someone charmed the monstrous cavern, growing wider in diameter the further my eyes traveled upward so that the fighting spirit lingered in the air?

Whatever it was, I was digging it. Things had certainly quieted down, giving me a real chance to get a feel for everything without being quite so overwhelmed. It was only now, as I took it all in, that I realized someone had charmed the ceiling. We were underground, yes, but the top of the beehive showed me stars—thousands of them. Bright, beautiful stars, the kind you're only fortunate enough to see once you escaped the bright lights of the city. Even then, these were breathtaking. I was finally able to forget about Darius when I looked at those stars, twinkling bright white and yellow—and pink and amber, the longer I watched. Stunning.

While I knew Zayne's sanctuary extended outward from the hive area—into what, I had no idea: the ground?—there was still plenty to take in here. I appreciated the openness now that I was away from all those winding levels. From the tower, I couldn't see a soul, though I felt the hum of nighttime activity all around me. It was a contemplative, strong sort of busyness that you get when everyone is working in tandem.

My gaze wandered lower, to the base level of the hive, upon which the castle—the headquarters of Zayne's militia—sat. While the castle itself was a sprawling, reaching piece of black gothic architecture, like a building straight out of a freakin' Tim Burton movie, its grounds were rather beautiful. Street lamps emitting a soft yellow glow dotted the cobblestone paths, paired with a series of lush green hedge mazes that seemed to breathe and shiver out of the corner of my eye whenever I wasn't looking directly at them. The lamps continued into the green passages, and I blinked hard, wondering if my mind was playing tricks on me when I swore I saw the maze rearrange itself.

Right. Definitely *not* going in there anytime soon.

Distant voices carried up to me as I continued my somewhat lazy observation of the world within a world, the stress I'd felt after a restless sleep easing away since I'd found a Darius-less rooftop some fifteen minutes earlier. The stress levels spiked up again, however, when I realized those voices belonged to two figures I knew—two male figures strolling around in front of the castle's courtyard just in front of the entrance to the maze.

"Fuckers," I whispered, leaning forward and squinting somewhat. Here I'd spent the whole day alone, wondering where *both* my boys had scampered off to, and there they were, going for a midnight walk and having a casual chat while they were at it.

Like two old friends.

My brows furrowed. Did Zayne and Darius know each other?

I shook my head. No. No, there wasn't some grand conspiracy theory unraveling around me—they were just going for a walk together.

*Yeah, because they'd seemed like the best of pals earlier,* the negative Nancy of my inner voices protested.

So, while I hated to snoop on two people I cared about—spying on Ravena and Darius had just seemed like smart practice, honestly—I called upon my more heightened hearing. You know, just to confirm that my worst fears were nothing more than products of a tired mind and an overactive imagination.

"...don't understand why you had to just leave her," I heard Darius say—grumble, more like. The distance between us was too great for me to get a perfect read, but I could make out the words with what I assumed was a decent level of accuracy. There was a slight pause, and I caught the two staring at each other, expressions hard, as Darius added, "Why not just tell her the truth? Kaye deserves that much."

I almost hopped out right then and there. Maybe I didn't

*want* to know. Maybe it was better I just let it go and grill Darius about it later.

Or...

I refocused my listening in and cushioned my mid-section with my arms as I leaned over the railing, honing in on the pair as they meandered around an otherwise empty courtyard. Although I had missed what my brother had said to Darius's last question, I was able to catch the end of another one.

"Why leave at all?"

"My father summoned me to Alfheim," Zayne told him, and maybe I was just looking for something that wasn't there, but I swore I heard a pang of regret in his voice. "I couldn't refuse him. He wanted to teach me everything he knew, everything he hadn't told me while I was growing up. I didn't want to leave Kaye, but I had to. If I hadn't, I'd be nowhere near ready to fight Abramelin today."

My eyes narrowed slightly, the knot in my stomach looping around itself once more. It was uncomfortable listening to two people you cared about talking *about* you, and my cheeks prickled with color—embarrassed, guilty color.

*No.* I shook my head. I had a right to know all this stuff, all this information my own flesh and blood had kept from me since I was a teenager. If this was the only way to learn it, then I could forgive myself for eavesdropping.

"This Abramelin guy sounds like a real gem," Darius said through what sounded like gritted teeth. I couldn't blame him. I obviously hated the ArchMage because he had tried to kill me— twice—but now that we knew he was after shifters and their sympathizers? I was surprised Darius hadn't flipped his lid and gone rogue.

"He wants to annihilate your kind," Zayne told him, "but I suspect he always knew he couldn't do that without outraging a very large part of the supernatural community."

Darius offered a cold chuckle. "Nice to know you guys *do* give a shit about us."

"The minority opinion has to scream the loudest to be heard," Zayne said, and I swore I caught him rolling his eyes. "Bigots are found in all communities, shifters too. But now they have a sword at the helm of their prejudices, and if we don't act fast, he'll continue his rampage of terror and destruction until there is nothing left."

"So why go after people like Kaye?"

"If supernatural sympathizers are out of the way," my brother explained after a brief pause, his momentary silence making me uneasy, "then he can attack shifters without anyone there to stop him."

"Hey." The pair stopped walking, and I caught Darius planting a hand on my brother's chest. While they were both tall men, Zayne had stayed a beanpole well into his adult years. Wiry and slender—it was a frame that worked well for fae speed. Darius's massive hand nearly covered the breadth of his chest. "Shifters have power too, you know. We aren't just a bunch of animals. We have strength, speed, healing abilities—"

"But no magic," Zayne countered, "and magic is what will save us from Abramelin and his minions. Unfortunately, as mighty as *many* shifter clans are, your Sanctius clan included, you cannot wield magic."

"It's what makes us second-class citizens," my dragon said, his voice a half-snarl that made the hairs on my arms stand up. I rubbed them quickly, willing the goosebumps to disappear.

"It's what makes the fight unfair," Zayne stressed with a sigh. "It's why we need each other if we want to survive this."

Both had a point, of course. It wasn't fair for a supernatural race to attack shifters simply to avenge the unfortunate murders of a few people. Not that I approved of innocents being slaughtered, but Abramelin was taking his vendetta above and beyond. If what Zayne said was correct, the ArchMage was gearing up for a full-on genocide, and my brother's militia, all the creatures working in the beehive around me, was the only thing standing in the way.

Fleetingly, I wondered if Abramelin had any idea that I was Zayne's sister. Because apparently, my brother was a *huge* thorn in the guy's side, and if Abramelin wanted to hurt him, assassinating his family—those that were still alive, that is—this would probably be a pretty good way to go about it.

I bit my lip, wondering if Zayne was the real reason I had been dragged into all of this. Maybe it wasn't that I sympathized with shifters at all. Maybe it was just because we'd been in the same womb for nine months of our lives.

"So why do this for us?" Darius asked, his voice dragging me out of my thoughts. "You can't be doing all this, endangering your life, just because you aren't some asshole who thinks shifters are dogs."

"No, of course not." Zayne sniffed as if the very question insulted him. I didn't recognize that part of him—this uppity, somewhat regal war general he had become. I missed the goofy, silly Zayne, the one who built blanket forts with me and glared down guys in high school when they wouldn't take a hint.

"So? What is it? What's pushing you to help us?"

"My loyalties to shifters run as deep as my heart beats strong."

I frowned. Since when? I grew up with the opinions that I had of the other supernatural and shifter races because my brother and aunt had instilled a strong sense of tolerance and acceptance within me. That being said, I hadn't ever known Zayne to have any special affiliations with shifters beyond not being a horrendous ass to them: that was the case with most of the fairies I knew when I was young.

"She's always been different from you," Darius started, but my brother cut him off curtly.

"And I've never loved her any less for it," he insisted. "I'm many things, but I'm *not* my father. Not entirely, anyway."

*What the hell...?*

I wiggled a finger in my ear, just to see if maybe I was hearing things wrong, but my heightened senses seldom failed me. Was Darius referring to me? That I was different?

How? My chest tightened, and I suddenly found myself blinking furiously to keep the tears at bay. I wasn't someone to burst into tears over nothing, either. But listening in on this conversation... It had tapped something buried within me, something I hadn't even realized I'd care about at this stage in my life. *Of course,* Zayne's abandonment screwed me up, but no worse than my fathers did. And here they were, my two guys, talking about it so casually, like it was nothing.

"I wasn't sure how to tell her why she couldn't come with me," Zayne admitted solemnly, and I swiped the back of my hand under my nose, sniffling. "How do you break that to someone? She was just a kid. It seemed easier at the time to just go."

*Easier for you...* No amount of blinking would stop the floodgates from bursting anymore, and I just let the tears flow. I'd always wondered how Zayne would rationalize what he did to me —how he left his little sister behind, on her own, after our dad had done the exact same thing years earlier. And to hear that he just figured it was easier to ghost out on me, to disappear one day without a trace—it *really* hurt.

And that was putting it mildly. Each word was like a knife to the heart, and by the time he fell quiet, there were too many knives, too many serrated edges, to the point where I could barely hold myself up. I wanted nothing more than to collapse and hide away behind the balcony ledge, to sit there and bawl my eyes out until there was nothing left. I'd done it once before, after all. I was due for a good sobbing, given all the bullshit that had rained down on me over the last few weeks.

But I stayed strong. Barely holding myself up, sure, but I kept listening.

"I'll tell her everything," Zayne said, and I watched him turn back when he undoubtedly realized Darius was no longer strolling along beside him. They'd been walking in a large loop around the courtyard for the whole conversation, clearly out there, far from council chambers and castle bedrooms, so they could have this very personal, very cutting, conversation about me without anyone else hearing.

"When?" my dragon demanded.

"When the fighting's over," Zayne told him. "There's too much going on for me to pick at those scars."

They weren't scars. I hadn't ever fully *healed*. They were gaping sores, blistering wounds, that had temporarily closed over the years, ones that were ready to pop open at the slightest provocation.

"That's not good enough," I heard Darius say through the hazy fog of a full-on emotional meltdown clouding my senses. It was coming. I could feel it. Darius's voice sounded muffled as I slowly lost control on my heightened senses, struggling to stay with the pair below. "You owe Kaye more than that."

"What do you want from me?" Zayne snapped, his voice fading, fading, fading from me as I started to fold in on myself. "I'm trying to fight a madman here. I'm trying to manage all these people. I'm trying..."

*Not hard enough.* He might have had a million things going on in his life, but if I didn't get the truth—whatever that might be, a truth that apparently even *Darius* knew—then I would never forgive him.

"Fuck this." Pushing myself away from the balcony railing, I stalked through my bedroom and rushed through the castle with a push of fae speed. To those I passed on the way, I was a blur, just another shadow in a building full of them, captured in the torchlight and built-in electronic pod lights alike. I pushed myself hard, not wanting Zayne and Darius to get away, not wanting them to forget this rather devastating conversation that I'd forced myself to endure.

Because I needed answers. I needed them *now*—not when the fighting was over, not when Abramelin was dead, not when his band of horrible cronies was defeated.

Right. Fucking. Now.

"Hey!" I shouted, feeling a grim sense of satisfaction when both men jumped at the sound of my voice cracking across the otherwise silent courtyard. They both stopped and turned toward me as I approached, my slippered feet pounding the cobblestone. All around, the street lamps flickered, my emotion leaving my personal magic unchecked—to the point, it was playing with the lights. I took a deep breath before stopping in front of them, my hands clenched in tight fists, and tried to steady myself with deep breathing.

It was *not* effective. This was why I didn't do yoga.

"Kaye, is everything okay—"

"Don't start with me," I snapped as I cut Darius off, raising a finger to him. "You and I are going to have a serious talk. But first. *You*," I faced my big brother, glaring, "have a lot of explaining to do, and I'm not leaving until I get some answers."

His red eyebrows knitted together, but the flush of color in his cheeks was an obvious giveaway; I'd all but caught him in the act.

"Kaye, what are you talking about?" He reached out to touch my arm. I stiffened at the contact and he hastily retracted his hand, almost as if I'd burned him. "Did you have a nightmare? Do you still get those?"

"Don't try to change the subject," I snapped, positively bristling. "I heard you two talking." My head bobbed up and down feverishly at the slight eye-widening from both of them. "Yeah, that's right. I listened in. I couldn't sleep, so I was out on the balcony and I saw you two...."

"There's a lot you don't know," Zayne told me. He sounded more defensive than I would have liked, which only turned my stare steelier. "If you just caught snippets... Kaye, listening in on people's conversations is *rude*."

"Don't lecture me. You're not my father. You and him both bailed on me, and now I've learned it was so you could hang out together." I gestured to the immense cavern around us, the walls seeming so vast and sprawling from the very base level of the hive. "Was it here? Did he bring you here all those years ago? Is that why you both left me alone to fend for my fucking self? What *truth* do I need to know?"

As I sucked in a strangled gasp, I suddenly realized I was crying again. Not a full-tilt sob-fest, but my voice quivered with emotion and my vision blurred with tears. I hoped neither of the two men staring at me could tell, but from the way Zayne's expression softened—and Darius's darkened as though he wanted to cradle me to him and fend off the world with his bare hands—I knew that was just a pipe dream. If either suggested I go inside to calm down, however, I was going to inflict some serious damage.

"I need to know," I said, forcing my voice to quiet in an effort to hide the fact that it was quivering. The tactic sort of worked, though I sounded breathier now. My eyes closed briefly when Darius placed a hand on my upper back, spreading it wide, its warmth soothing. Slowly, I drew in a breath and lifted my gaze to Zayne, who studied me with that same pained expression he'd worn earlier when we were first reunited. I didn't like seeing it, but if it meant he would tell me what I needed to hear, I'd take it. Swallowing hard, I held his gaze steadily and cleared my throat. "I think I deserve to know. Zayne. This is my life. My whole life. You owe me after..."

After totally abandoning me to go hang out with the man who had abandoned us *both* years earlier.

"You know she's right," Darius added gruffly. I resisted the urge to pin him with a glare.

"I can speak for myself," I said over my shoulder. His hand fell away from my back as he added a bit of distance between our bodies. Despite everything going on in my mind, I found myself missing the heat of his touch.

"Kaye, there's so much going on—"

"I'm your *sister*," I argued. I then blinked hard so the gathering tears would fall. While I didn't enjoy watching him suffer, it was almost as if there was this little creature inside of me who did. Zayne might have felt guilty for leaving me behind, for keeping all these secrets from me, but this was my first and possibly only opportunity to actually *see* it. I didn't want to be cruel, but for my own sanity, I almost needed to know he hurt just as badly as I had all those years ago.

Zayne cursed under his breath, then looked away, face momentarily twisted with a blend of frustration and sadness. I moved in, sliding my hand into his—so much cooler than Darius's—and squeezing hard.

"Please?"

He looked away a moment longer, and though I couldn't see his whole face, I could see enough to watch the internal struggle, the back-and-forth debate. Finally, he shook his head and sighed, then stared me dead in the eye.

"You want the whole truth?"

I nodded and pulled my hand back. "And nothing but the truth."

"So help you, God," Darius finished for us. He smirked when I shot him an exasperated look over my shoulder. The twist of his lips and the glimmer in his eye forced a half-smile out of me, try as I might to stop it.

"Fine," Zayne said, rolling up his sleeves and throwing his neck side to side—like he was getting ready for a fight. I winced at the crackling sound, then realized I had a habit of cracking my neck like that too. When he was through, my brother met my gaze again, eyebrows lifted, and asked, "You sure?"

"*Yes.*"

"Because it's a lot to handle right now," he stated. "I've tried like hell to keep this from you because I know it'll hurt. Just remember that."

"I deal with this kind of stuff every single day with clients. I'm due for a bit of it in my own life." Or so I hoped. Helping clients manage crisis after crisis was one thing, but we psychologists were always terrible at handling breakdowns within our own lives. It was why so many in my field were clueless when it came to their own flaws.

"Right, so you know our mother is fae," he started, and I gave him my best *no duh* look. He shook his head. "Okay, okay, okay... So. Before you were born, me, our mother, and my father lived a pretty easy life. No problems. For the most part, we were happy... or so I thought."

My eye twitched. I hadn't missed the fact that he'd said *our* for mom and *my* for dad.

"Then we learn that Mom had an affair," Zayne continued, tempering his tone with me like he was telling a kid that Santa Claus wasn't real. I crossed my arms as a pulse of jumbled feeling tore through me at the news. I'd never met my mom, as she died giving birth to me, but I'd always hoped she was a good, kind person. But I guess it shouldn't have surprised me to learn she'd been unfaithful; so many fae strayed during relationships.

"Did you find out with who?" I asked in the silence that followed, then looked quickly between Zayne and Darius. Both stared back at me like I was missing something, so I cleared my throat and added, "Someone... you knew?"

"Not really," Zayne admitted. "I never met him, but I know Mom had fallen in love with him. The... The affair resulted in you. Kaye, we... We don't share a father. We aren't whole siblings. Technically, you're my half-sister."

Darius reacted first when my knees finally did buckle, and I gripped his arm as he steadied me, finding solace in his warmth, in his hard figure propping me up. I should have had a thousand racing thoughts, yet my mind felt like it was steeped in a dense fog that I just couldn't penetrate. Try as I might, I couldn't collect my words to form any coherent questions—or thoughts, or feelings, or *anything*. Numb—that was the term for it. In shock. I'd seen it all the time with clients. I'd seldom ever felt it myself.

"There's more," Zayne told me, voice wavering. "Kaye, this man that Mom had the affair with... He... Well, he..."

It wasn't like my brother to stammer. My narrowed eyes darted up to him, and in a voice stronger than I felt, even as Darius held me up with an arm around my waist, I demanded he just spit it out already.

"Why freeze up now?" I snapped. "Just tell me, Zayne. It can't be any worse than the fact that you and I aren't technically brother and sister."

"Of course we are," he insisted, swooping in on me and cradling my face in both of his hands. Darius's hold on me tightened. The claustrophobia of being sandwiched between these two men was overwhelming, yet I had no desire to shove either of them away. While the doubt within me insisted that they'd deserve the cold shoulder, the other little voice, the one that *always* steered me right, rightly assured me that they did all of this out of love.

Logically, I could accept that.

From a snap-judgement, more emotional standpoint... I'd probably need some time.

"Kaye, I've loved you from the day you were born to—"

"You mean the day I killed your mother?" I whispered, eyes welling with tears again. His face screwed with pain, but he took a deep breath and schooled his features better than I would have had our places been reversed.

"*Our* mother," he murmured, easing away and giving me space to catch my breath. "She was our mother. She loved you. I've always loved you. Father..." He bit his lip and wouldn't meet my eye. "He left because he couldn't live with the child of his wife's affair. We've fought about it many times, but that won't change what he did."

It might not, but in that moment, I loved Zayne for going up to bat for me against the guy who abandoned his dead wife's daughter. I threw my shoulders back before carefully extracting myself from Darius's grasp. I had to stand on my own two feet for this.

"So, is that it? Is that the truth?" I asked as I wiped under my eyes, collecting unfallen tears with a sniffle. "That I'm the child of an affair?"

My brother studied me for a long moment as if trying to assess whether I was ready for the rest. I must have looked more capable of handling this than I felt because as I tried to ask again, he spoke the words that would shatter my reality into a million pieces.

"Kaye. The man Mom had an affair with... He was a shifter." He paused for a beat. "A dragon shifter."

There went the knees again. Both men tried to catch me, but Darius beat Zayne to the punch again. Everything just went blank—more shock, more high-pitched ringing in my ears. As Darius steadied me, I realized I couldn't feel my hands, but pressing them to my thighs told me they were cold and clammy.

*I... I was part shifter?*

Kids had always joked that I wasn't full fae, but I chalked it up to the fact that I got hips, boobs, and butt before any of them and they were jealous. Not because...

Supernaturals could sense other supernaturals.

And shifters.

Had everyone known but me? Was my genetic signature plain for the world to see, and they all just politely ignored it?

"I need to sit down," I muttered, and Darius half-carried me —my legs were moving, but I couldn't be sure if my feet even touched the ground—toward a bench near the mouth of the maze. He helped me settle, then crouched in front of me, as if ready to catch me should I faint and pitch forward, head-first, into the cobblestone below.

"Kaye?" My dragon's brows lifted slightly as he assessed me. While he didn't ask it, I knew he was trying to gauge whether I was okay.

And, of course, I wasn't.

"I need a second," I managed.

"Take all the time you need." He held up his hands and rocked back on his heels, adding some space between us—space

I didn't really want, honestly. I did, however, want distance from Zayne, especially when he strolled over and took a seat on the bench next to me. I positively bristled at the feel of him beside me, and although it was petulant, I got up and moved down to the end of the bench, crossed my arms, and turned my back on him. Anger roiled within me, churning with the grief of rehashing my mom's death and the now even more painful abandonment by my dad. And now... Now I wasn't even fully part of a culture, a family, I'd grown up in? I had always identified with the fae community. They were my rock, my home, my backbone when things got tough.

They had always accepted me, my sisters. Belladonna loved me like I was both a friend and a daughter. Now, there was this whole separate community that technically I was a part of, all because my mom had an affair. My true father had never come looking for me. Honestly, in that moment, it felt like I'd never actually had a father-figure in my life—period. After all, Dad bailed on me. Sperm-donor Dad never bothered to check on me.

*Maybe he didn't know.*

And that made it worse. I tried to shut off that little voice, the one that sounded louder than the others. My eyes shot open wide. That little voice. It had always been there...

Although I couldn't confirm it, shifters were said to have internal dialogues with their other forms. Was that little voice... my inner dragon? Could I shift? I couldn't even *fly*. What a pair we made, Darius and me.

"Kaye..." Zayne's voice interrupted what was bound to be a downward spiral, and I spared the barest of glances over my shoulder at him. He sighed, his arm stretched out along the back of the bench—but to his credit, he hadn't inched toward me since I'd moved away.

"What, Zayne?"

"I was just a kid when all this happened," he told me. "I heard Mom and Dad fighting about it after we found out she was pregnant. I didn't…I didn't know what to make of it then, and I struggle with it now."

"I'm sure you do," I remarked dryly.

"Mom found out I'd overheard everything," my brother continued, "and she begged me not to tell you. You were only a half-shifter. There was no telling if you'd even have the genes necessary to fully shift. It could have been seventy-thirty fae to shifter. We didn't know. We didn't want to burden you with this unnecessarily."

"Burden," I heard Darius scoff slightly, and I had to agree. It wasn't a burden to be a shifter. Well, from a political and social standpoint, maybe. Sighing, I faced Zayne and shook my head.

"I had a right to know who I am," I stated, "and *what* I am."

"I know." He placed a hand on my knee. "You're right. I'm so sorry it had to come out like this. I'm sorry for everything."

Unfortunately for my big brother, just saying the words wasn't enough. I heard them, of course. I saw the pain in his face, the tense twitch in his cheek. The psychologist in me deduced that the apology was genuine, but I just couldn't accept it. Not after all this time. All these years of lies. It wasn't like Zayne had spent years not telling me I had a bad haircut. Hiding my heritage from me was something that couldn't be swept under the rug and forgotten about with a simple apology.

I'd need time and space to sort through my muddled feelings. Right now, however, I was about two seconds away from blowing a fuse and unleashing a verbal hell on anyone within a ten-foot radius, so it was best that I just excused myself.

He called out for me as I pushed off the bench and jogged back toward the castle, but I only slowed when three figures rushed out the entryway I'd used earlier. They barreled by me, not breaking their stride, and shouted for Zayne. The alarm on their features made me stop, and as I whirled back, I discovered why.

"Abramelin's men have almost breached the portal!" one of

the men shouted, a fairy with jet black hair and elven features. "We've been trying to hold them off—"

Before he could finish, an explosion rocked through the underground sanctuary, rattling the beehive like a great earthquake. I cried out as the ground trembled and knocked me right on my ass. In my peripheral, I caught Darius racing straight for me, only to duck out of the way when chunks of magical ceiling, still glittering with a starry night sky, plummeted down and slammed into the castle's courtyard. More screams thundered from the upper levels as an alarm started to blare; it made me think of those natural disaster sirens, the ones alerting people to stay inside, to get to safety, to run.

All of which, I thought as I dove out of the way from more falling debris, was pretty damn good advice. Because seconds later, another explosion rocked the hive—only this time it radiated from somewhere within.

❧ 14 ☙

*FIREWORKS.* It all looked like the most impressive firework display I had ever seen in my life. Blasts of red, blue, purple, green—they twirled and zoomed across the hive's immense cavern. Whizzing, soaring, crackling. Majestic and beautiful. Vibrant and entertaining.

Only real fireworks didn't cause monumental damage when they slammed into something. Because these weren't fireworks. As I did an awkward crab-walk back until I hit the wall of the castle, I noted that these were bursts of magic. *Spellwork.* There were probably a few hexed items lobbed across the hive. It was absolute chaos. The vortex of *feeling*, the hurricane inside my head, had been transplanted to the real world—and it wasn't pretty.

If I didn't know better, I would have said that this was an invasion.

And it was. It had to be: gargoyles poured into the hive from the doorways on the top level, singing their terrible song of death, swarming together like a band of locusts before plunging down toward the castle. I shrieked when another chunk of the overhead slammed into the cobblestone some ten feet from me, the ground rumbling in the aftershocks of that first quake. I gritted my teeth at the sound of growls pealing through the air – the monsters were out, and as usual, they wanted blood.

"Darius!" I called for my dragon, but the crackling of magic combined with gargoyle roars and frightened screams drowned me out. Smoke had started to fill the courtyard—smoke that had a distinctly magical quality to it. Trying not to panic, I shook my head and stood in an effort to see over it, as I coughed. They were literally trying to smoke us out. *Bastards.* Squinting, I scanned the area for Darius and my brother, calling both their names and getting no response back. Dark shapes shot through the rising smoke, accompanied by the sounds of grunts and groans, a fight breaking out somewhere I couldn't see.

Abramelin's men must have found another way into Zayne's sanctuary. They couldn't all be coming from the main door I'd been escorted through earlier today.

My momentary search, a distraction more than anything else, left me vulnerable, and seconds later a force with the strength of a charging wildebeest knocked me off my feet. I cried out, pain radiating from the side where I'd been hit—like a direct shot to a kidney.

"Fuck..." I groaned. Not only had something invisible slammed into me, but I'd landed hard on my shoulder too. The pain seeped in from both sides, and just as I tried to stand, a massive hand worked into my hair, and dragged me across the cobblestone. Flailing, I did my best to ignore the searing burn in my scalp as I twisted around to get a better look at my attacker. While the fog obscured him, I could tell he was humanoid in appearance, pale like death, and wore all black.

*Demon or vampire.*

No surprise there that they crept into the hive in the dead of night.

Just as he started to lift me—by the root of my hair, no less— I snagged the curved knife off his belt, pleased that it had a jagged edge, and buried it deep in his meaty thigh. The creature emitted a high-pitched roar, his eyes glowing angrily, and dropped me. A burst of fae speed had me on my feet in a flash.

*Demon.* The blood red eyes gave him away, along with the skeletal face, his alabaster skin stretched thin over the bones. His blood encrusted horns curved over his head, and I winced at the sight of him.

"Son of a bitch," I spat, my face twisted with disgust. With one hand, I called forth a near-blinding flash of pure white light, then finally shoved him back with a pulse of energy that sent him stumbling. Unfortunately, it didn't knock him down quite like I wanted. As he twisted around to face me, first with his legs, then the top half of his body—like they weren't connected, his red eyes gleamed out of the darkness, a hunger in their depths that both chilled me, and sent streaks of lightning through my blood.

Then, while maintaining full eye contact, the demon ripped the knife from his thigh and ran his tongue along the blade.

To my further disgust, he spat a mouthful of brownish demon blood at me. Most of it missed, but I felt the cold splatter on my legs—like the icy fingers of death.

*Fucking demons.*

He lunged for me, knife in hand, his burly arms reaching for me, but this time I was ready. No more cheap shots when I wasn't looking.

I sidestepped his advance, twisting out of the way with all the grace of a prima ballerina—for the first time in my life. Apparently, I could get this body moving, half-shifter or not, when it really mattered. The demon snarled and turned back, his upper body whipping around before the lower half caught up, and I grimaced. This was why I'd never entertained demons in my day-to-day life: gross. as. fuck.

My gaze stayed steadfast to the blade, and I was soon able to pick up something of a pattern in my opponent's fighting style. Stab, stab, swipe. Stab to my right, my left, then try to swipe across my body. When he tried to impale my left, right on schedule, I clamped down on his arm and dragged him forward, managing to throw him off balance just enough to hoist him up and flip him over my shoulder. He slammed onto the cobblestone with a grunt, but managed to dodge my slippered foot when I tried to slam it down on his face. The blade swiped at my ankle, but I leapt out of the way. A faint whoosh of air ghosted across my skin, signaling just how close I'd been to being sliced open somewhere with an abhorred demon knife.

Rumor had it that just one cut, no bigger than a papercut, from a demon's blade would induce immediate necrosis of the surrounding skin.

No thanks. Not today, you disgusting evil bastard.

Unfortunately, while I'd managed to dodge the demon's blade, his free hand snaked out and slammed into the back of my knee, instantly buckling it. I cried out as I toppled down onto him, only *just* managing to roll over him rather than land on his mass of bones covered in ghostly white skin and black cloth rags. His knife came down, seemingly out of nowhere, and I rolled again and again and again, each time the blade landing hard on the ground rather than in my stomach. A burst of fae speed got me to my feet, but the demon was close behind. His red eyes narrowed as we assessed each other. I was faster, sure, but he seemed totally not fazed by the fact he was bleeding out from the wound I'd made on his thigh.

Could demons die? I hadn't the faintest idea, but I was ready to test my theory if it meant getting away from this creep.

I crouched down and raised my hands in a defensive stance. While pain still pulsed from where he'd slammed into me earlier —along with my throbbing shoulder and skinned knees—I was ready for the next round.

"Bring it," I barked, hands warming as I called upon a ball of white magic to form in the palm of each. "You may not like what I have to say this time around..."

His smile made me want to gag: slobbery yellow drool, like bile, oozed out between a set of jagged teeth. *Ugh*. The demon tossed the blade back and forth between his hands, then lifted it in the air and roared—the beginning of his charge. I tensed, my white magic orbs practically searing my skin.

But the demon never made it to me.

Instead, two steps later, a surge of blue flame engulfed him and fried him to a crisp. I withdrew my white magic and ducked down, shielding my face from the burn.

A burn that, all things considered, should have been much worse.

I closed my eyes tight. I was part dragon, after all. A regular fae probably couldn't get this close to a dragon's blaze and walk away unsinged. Darius's roar, ten times that of the demon's, made me look up sharply, and I found him some twenty feet away in all his exquisite dragon glory, a vampire under each front foot trying to wriggle free. The demon, meanwhile, was nothing more than a pile of ash. Scowling, I crawled forward, and with a summoning of a gentle breeze, dispersed the creature's ashes on the wind until he was nothing but scattered dust particles.

Out of the corner of my eye, Darius silenced the two screeching vampires, one right after the other—by removing their heads, which he then spat out. I watched one roll by me, mouth still open in a petrified scream, until it too dissolved to dust. You could only kill a vampire in a few different ways: stake to the heart or a good beheading were the preferred choices. Sunlight and fire worked too, and while there was no sun in the hive, only a manic rainbow of magic bursts paired with flood-lights pouring down from all the different levels leading up to the top, we certainly had fire.

Jumping up, I covered my head and ran for Darius when the broken remains of a gargoyle plummeted down onto the court-yard. He reached out for me, that huge head steering me toward him. A few of the spiny bits sticking off his face poked my back, but I'd already started to mentally block out the pain where I could.

Head turned back, he assessed me through one eye as I

shielded myself between his massive shoulder and the base of his scaly neck from the absolute magical mess imploding around us. When he snorted at me, smoke shooting out his nostrils, and gave an eye twitch, I nodded.

"Fine," I told him. "I'm okay. Demon just got the jump on me. No serious harm done."

He snorted again, this time a little softer, and then nudged me—and nudged, and nudged, and nudged, until it became clear he was trying to herd me toward something.

"Stop," I ordered sharply, pushing him away. If I knew Darius, he was about two seconds away from picking me up by the scruff of my robe, which flapped open freely now, and carrying me. One look in the direction he was trying to send me and I knew what he wanted: there was a tunnel big enough for his dragon form to fit behind the castle. On my tour earlier, Eilie had told me it led to some undeveloped caverns—ones that eventually brought you back to upper Alfheim. I shook my head when he huffed at me, this time his mouth illuminating with blue flame behind his teeth.

"No," I told him. "Absolutely not. We're not running. We have to find Zayne. We have to..." I licked my lips, at a loss for words. "I don't know. Protect people!"

While everyone here was technically part of the militia, I'd seen plenty of supernatural folk today who were clearly here for their building prowess or their brain—magical ability and brain just hadn't factored in to their presence. I wasn't about to leave them to die, not when I could defend them from the goons Abramelin sent to squash the resistance. Not a chance in hell.

My hands fell to my hips when I caught Darius rolling his freakin' dragon eyes at me. Behind, his tail flicked hard to the side suddenly, pinning a goblin between it and the wall. The creature groaned as green blood gurgled out its mouth, and it lay motionless when Darius dropped it.

"We're not going anywhere," I stated. "I don't know where Zayne is, but we're staying and helping him fight."

Another eye-roll.

"And you can cut the attitude, Mister." I poked his neck as hard as I could. "Right now, you're one of the best weapons here, so suck it up and go fry some bad guys."

Huh. Who would have thought I'd be ordering a dragon back *in* to the madness? If I had a lick of sense, I'd take the out Darius offered and hightail it out of there. Maybe, somehow, I could get back to the surface level and rally some more fighting forces.

Although, according to Eilie, many "neutral" supernaturals weren't too keen on throwing their hat into this fight and challenge Abramelin. Maybe if they saw the carnage in the hive, they might change their tune. People always shy away from a fight when they think it doesn't affect them. Little do they know, Abramelin's poison will seep into their souls too—all they had to do was wait and let him continue unchecked.

No. We weren't going to run. We were going to fight.

After barreling through a squadron of goblins, me using my fae speed to knock them off balance—once from the right, once from the left, using the smoke billowing around the lower level to hide my attack—and Darius charring them to bits, we headed for the next rung of the outer floors. It was chaos everywhere, not just around the castle. Bursts of magic, beautiful for a moment, continued to rock the sanctuary, knocking stone from the walls and shattering the balconies overlooking the structure. The outer levels were nothing more than one long, winding ramp that worked its way around the edge of the hive. Waist-high walls would keep you from tumbling over the side, but I'd already heard a handful of shrieks as supernaturals tumbled over the edge from the upper levels, plummeting toward broken bones.

Or death on impact. I tried to reach out and catch one—a young fae who couldn't have been more than eighteen—but she was *just* out of reach. The look on her face, the fear and shock of weightlessness as she fell, would forever haunt me. I watched her go, arms hanging out into the aerial combat zone, fingers outstretched and grasping for her. She didn't have wings. Like me, she couldn't fly. All she could do was fall.

She disappeared into the smoke growing across the ground level. One moment she was there, the next gone, engulfed in darkness. The clamor down the way from us brought me back to the fight, with Darius behind me, a grim determination in his eye that encouraged me to keep going. This was what I'd signed up for, after all. Death. Destruction. War. He gave me an out and I chose to stay.

I had to learn to stomach it all—and fast. Clearing my throat, I took a deep breath and hurried on, heading straight for the source of the shouting. Darius plodded along after me, cramped. The walkway was only *just* big enough for him to fit through, and the ceiling overhead of the pathway on the next level kept scraping his head.

At least I couldn't hear him complain in dragon form. Bolstering my courage, I threw myself into the fray.

"Get back inside!" I shouted at a pair of dwarves trying to stab at the vampires on the other side of a door. Six vamps appeared to be trying to pry the door open, the dwarves trying to keep it shut. From the smell, I guessed that door led to the kitchens. No real fighters in there.

I pressed up against the wall as Darius shot forth a stream of blue flame. A few of the vampires managed to dodge it, running up the walls and flattening themselves on the ceiling while their companions writhed in agony before turning to dust. Before I could finish the vamps off, the two dwarves struck out with surprising speed, impaling both bloodsuckers with their kitchen knives before retreating inside. Two more piles of dust for me to walk through.

Not that I wanted to. It would be easy to demonize all the creatures fighting for Abramelin in the heat of the moment: goblins, trolls, gargoyles, vampires, and real demons alike. But as I pressed onward, Darius squishing along behind me, I realized these stereotypically "evil" creatures weren't the only ones fighting. I watched elves clash with nymphs, the night elves on our side and the typically rather sweet nymphs fighting for Abramelin, war paint smeared along their high cheekbones like the latest matte blush.

It wasn't until I reached the fourth level, having done what I could along the way to help all those in trouble, that I realized there were a few fae among Abramelin's crowd.

"What are you doing?" I cried. Behind me, Darius had clambered over the little balcony and leapt across the hive. In my peripheral, I caught him batting down a swarm of gargoyles before slamming into the walkways on the other side of the hive. The fae in question whirled around, blood on his teeth and a dead shifter at his feet.

I could only assume it was a shifter: the woman was naked with her throat slit. She must have changed back to her human form after she died.

"You're a strange one," the fairy remarked, his head cocked to one side as his ice-blue gaze swept up and down my figure. "A little underdressed for the party, but I think we'll make do."

"How can you side with him?" I demanded, and he laughed at the quiver in my voice. I swallowed down the emotion, not wanting him to see the weakness. "He's insane. You're killing good, innocent people."

"Shifter lovers?" The blond snorted and wiped his blooded hands on his beige dress shirt, opting to display the blood rather than hide it in his black dress pants. "They aren't *good* people. They're betraying their own kind."

My nose wrinkled. Hands curling to fists, it became quickly apparent that I wasn't going to get this guy on my side. "That's disgusting."

"You smell disgusting," he fired back without missing a beat. "Your scent... What's wrong with you? Are you sick?"

So, other fairies *could* sense that I was only half-fae. The others must have just had the decency to hide it from me all my life.

Perfect.

"You're the only one who is *sick*," I spat, cheeks flaming. "You're destroying your kin and clan—"

He pointed to the dead shifter at his feet. "*This* bitch wasn't my kin."

"We are all part of this world," I reasoned. "We should be protecting each other from this maniac, not—"

"Like hell I'm ever going to fight alongside filthy beasts." He sneered at me.

Before I could get another word in, he charged me, his fae speed making him nothing but a blur. As I dove out of the way, scrambling to stay on my feet, I realized he was a shadowmelder—a fairy who could lose themselves entirely in the shadows. Lucky for me, with all the magic explosions and obscenely bright floodlights everywhere, there were very few shadows for him to meld into. As I ducked down and landed a punch straight to his gut, Darius's roar rattled the hive. In my brief moment of distraction, my gaze searching him out, fearing he'd been hurt somehow, the blond fairy's fist slammed into my jaw. Pain radiated across my face, behind my eyes, and I staggered back, swallowing a cry.

"Too slow," he leered. "Whatever you are. You might look like one of my kind, but you most certainly aren't."

"No..." I used every ounce of fae speed I had when he ran at me, crouching low one half-second and shooting up into him the next. The blow threw him off balance, and just like the gargoyles at the train station, I took advantage of his momentum and shoved hard. He toppled over the edge of the walkway with a shout. As I straightened up and wiped a trickle of blood away from my split lower lip, I glared where he had last been standing. "I'm *not* one of your kind."

Laughter crept across my skin after I turned away, and I spun back, eyes wide, to find him hovering there on the other side of the railing, baby blue wings flapping. Fairy wings... Of course. I'd always been so jealous of them. To me, they were the most beautiful things in the world.

He didn't deserve them.

"Try harder next time, half-breed," he snarled. I only *just* managed to dodge the orb of white magic he threw at me, though I felt the heat of it singe my hair. It slammed into the wall behind me, cracking in and shattering a window. When I tried to retaliate, he was gone. Panting, I inched hesitantly toward the edge, but he was nowhere to be seen. Darius, meanwhile, moved quickly across the hive's cavernous center and squashed another gargoyle along the way, pinning the creature between his huge dragon form and my walkway's railing.

It snapped the creature in half, but I blitzed its head with white magic, just to be sure.

"You okay?" I called, poking my head out to get a better look at him. Dark blood, almost purple, oozed out from under one of his scales, but otherwise he seemed unharmed. He gave me a snort in response, then fried an oncoming trio of gargoyles. I exhaled softly, pleased. "Good."

After the fairy's attack, Darius seemed less inclined to leave my side—not that I minded, or anything. We moved up the pathways as a singular unit, helping all those we could along the way. There were many within the militia who were more than capable of holding up their end of a fight. At one point, somewhere on the fifth level, we passed a dryad who had summoned tree roots *through* the stone and used them to strangle their opponents. He offered a toothy grin and a wave as Darius and I passed. I'd stared at the twitching goblins ensnared in the roots, wide-eyed and thankful that the guy was on *our* side.

I couldn't be sure how long it took us to get to the top level. We faced a lot of heat on the way up: Darius wasn't exactly a subtle creature moving through the battlefield. His size made him the target of anything with wings, which he seemed more than happy to either fry or chomp out of the air. While I had a few bumps and bruises, my lower lip bloody and my temple bleeding, I was in relatively okay condition when we reached the top level—given this was my first ever epic battle and all.

Time slowed during our march to the top. They say a thirty-second fight feels like an hour, and today I learned ten times over that that was absolutely the case. Every skirmish I entered dragged on, when in reality it was a minute or two, at most. My opponent either gave up, faced Darius, or was rendered unconscious. My dragon was more inclined to kill. I just wanted them knocked out.

We had no game plan in mind, but after breaching the top floor, I realized that, whether we thought about it or not, we had come here with a purpose. Still no Zayne in sight, but I spied Abramelin's army puppet masters at a distance. Four warlocks in great black cloaks stood watching the whole thing, peering down at the vortex of magical chaos below—all four wearing identical smirks, as though this horrific battle was entertainment to them. Any supernatural who tried to flee through the main doors that led out to the other chambers were eviscerated by one of the four before they could get within ten feet of them.

"I think we just found our Big Boss," I muttered, resting against Darius's side, the pair of us as out of sight as we could be, given he was the size of a city bus. My dragon breathed heavier now, and every bone in my body screamed for rest.

But we couldn't give up now. Not when we'd finally found the assholes pulling the strings.

"Cross over and try to attack them from the other side," I instructed, wincing when one of the warlocks stunned a charging elf and then flung him over the side of the walkway. Down he fell, unable to flail, to scream—anything. How the hell was I going to do this? Gulping, I squared my shoulders and nodded toward the quartet. "While you've got their attention, I'll try to blitz by and take them out one at a time."

Darius huffed, the sound rumbling from deep within—he wasn't happy about it. I couldn't blame him, but what other choice did we have?

"I'll be fine," I insisted, though I didn't believe the words, not even as I said them. "Just try to keep them busy." Then, when he didn't immediately spring to action, I fist-pumped his enormous front foot and grinned. "We got this."

He rolled his eyes, and, thankfully, did as he was told. I watched from what little shadows there were as he moved from one side of the hive to the other. Given we were on the top level, the space between the two sides was larger, and my stomach twisted when he missed the top walkway and crashed down to the second. He managed to catch himself, but it wasn't until he started climbing up, tail swishing at the creatures trying to stab him from the second walkway, that I breathed a little easier.

Although his jump wasn't as elegant as I'm sure either of us would have liked, he succeeded in distracting the warlocks. All four studied him with pursed lips, expressions pinched in annoyance. Apparently, a massive dragon just wasn't an intimidating foe to these guys.

Arrogant dicks.

Inhaling and exhaling two deep breaths, I summoned my final reserves of fae speed and burst forth, racing down the walkway with the aim of catching the warlock closest to me off-guard.

That plan failed, spectacularly, when he turned and flicked his hand at me. Seconds later some invisible force, with the strength of a wrecking ball, slammed into me. I cried out as pain shot through my back and up my spine. Thankfully, I had a fucking stone wall to cushion my fall. I hit hard, the impact making my world spin for a few uncomfortable moments as I slid down to the floor.

Only I didn't have the luxury to recover. I now had the attention of two warlocks, who turned away from the chaos in the hive to focus entirely on me.

"You should have given in to the gargoyles when you had the chance, half-breed," one of the warlocks snapped, light reflecting off his greasy mop of long black hair. Had he gelled it down? Gotta look good before you can slaughter, apparently.

I bristled at the term, like my heritage was the greatest insult he could pay me, but refused to let it show.

"Fuck you," I spat.

The pair exchanged amused looks, chuckling.

"Look at the mouth on her. So typical of shifter bitches." The second warlock, his hair a flaming red and nose lined with fat freckles—each a different color, like body art. "I'm afraid, half-breed, that the gargoyles would have offered a less painful death than the one we have in mind."

A burst of Darius's flame caught all three of us off-guard, but the warlock nearest to him was more on the ball than I'd hoped. Before the fire reached any of them, he whirled around and threw up a shielding spell. The fire blasted against an invisible wall, which split the stream in half and rendered the warlocks totally unharmed. Even as Darius moved closer, the flame darkening to a brilliant navy blue, we could barely feel the heat of it on this side.

Not good.

Jumping on the distraction, I fired off two pulses of white magic at each warlock—which they deflected deftly with lazy flicks of their wrists. I tried everything in my arsenal: weather charms, Illumination strobes, energy pulses, transformation spells. The warlocks just seemed entertained with my efforts, deflecting and blocking whatever I threw their way until I had nothing left. The tank was empty, my energy depleted.

And then they had their fun. I had no words for the hex they used on me—all I knew was that it induced a pain so profound, so staggering, that I barely held onto my consciousness the second it hit me. I screamed, twisting and writhing on the ground, as they took turns blasting me with what felt like a magnified cattle prod. Each bolt sent agony surging through my body, straight down to the marrow. I had no thoughts, no fears, no plans to retaliate. All I had was pain unlike any I had ever known.

Pain and their laughter, skittering across my body and illuminating my steadily darkening mind.

For a few seconds, I welcomed death if it meant it would all stop.

That was until I heard Darius roar—but not as a dragon. Briefly, the torture ceased, and as I twisted my head to the side, mouth hanging open and an endless stream of tears rolling down my cheeks, my hazy vision honed in on a figure bursting into the fold.

Darius. In human form.

"D-Darius..." I tried to reach out to him, tried to tell him to turn back, that he was no match for their magic. But he breached the warlock's shield like it was nothing, and as my dragon pummeled that first warlock, I realized, my thought process still in bits and pieces, that it was because the shield was there to repel *magical* attacks. Shifters might not have magic, but a dragon's fire was as good as in the natural world. The shield wouldn't prevent a physical attack.

Stiff and unsteady, I twisted onto my side to watch. One warlock down, a mangled bloody heap of a man on the floor. The other tried to blast Darius with an onslaught of multi-colored spells, fast and furious in their conjuring, but my dragon dodged and ducked and dipped out of the way before tackling the man to the ground.

His attack was savage and merciless.

But as effective as it was, it was short-lived. As I'd predicted, he was no match for all four warlocks, and the two who had tormented me soon had my dragon contorting on the ground, pummeled with a pain hex so powerful that Darius coughed up a mouthful of blood.

"Filthy shifters," the greasy warlock sneered, spitting on Darius as he lay trembling on the ground. Unlike me, his eyes were still focused, fueled by rage, and he refused to stay down until one of the warlocks magically pinned him up against the wall, his naked body covered in a mix of sweat, blood, and dirt.

"Hate to break you two up," the freckled warlock insisted as he lunged for me, snatching my arm and dragging me to the edge of the walkway, "but I can only imagine what mongrels you would breed, given the chance. Consider this a mercy."

And then he tossed me over the railing and into the hive—like he was tossing a piece of garbage into the trash. A scream tore from my throat as I fell, my very life flashing before my eyes. I stared up at what was left of the enchanted ceiling, wishing the last thing I'd ever see wasn't a destroyed starry night sky, half-twinkling like a neon sign that had run out of juice.

My view became obstructed, not by bursts of magic or gargoyles—but by a dragon.

My dragon.

Darius flung himself over the ledge and plummeted after me, shifting right before my eyes to hasten his fall.

Time seemed to slow until it was just me and him, the rest of the world forgotten. The fear eased out of me, replaced by a quiet acceptance that once I hit the ground, I was dead. No wings to stop me. No power left to cushion my fall. Just me and the concrete, destined for the last date of my life. A beautiful sense of relief washed over me that Darius, of all the people in my life, would be the last thing I'd ever see. Not the fake stars. Not the explosions of battle. Darius—my dragon—in all his glory...

... coming to my rescue. Sacrificing himself for me.

I reached up as if to wave him away, to tell him to go back. He didn't need to do this. Not for me.

He responded with wings.

*His wings.*

They shot out from his back, practically spanning the entire width of the hive, and suddenly he was racing toward me faster than I was falling. I watched, mystified, as he flapped them hard twice before curling them in, gusts of wind like that of an oncoming tornado pummeling the walkways. People screamed—and Darius dived, shooting passed me. Seconds later, the wings shot out again, and I slammed hard onto his back, his spinal spikes stabbing hard into my skin.

And then the falling stopped. I blinked hard, wondering if this was death, only to quickly realize my descent had slowed.

Darius was flying. A strangled giggle crawled up my throat and burst out, and I rolled onto my stomach and held onto him with everything I had left.

My dragon had earned his wings back. I closed my eyes tight as I hugged him.

We still hit the ground hard, the impact loosening me and sending me tumbling off his back. The force blew away the billowing smoke around the castle, and when I pushed up onto my feet, the cobblestones taking a bit of skin off in the process, I found my dragon back in human form, motionless.

"Darius!"

My legs didn't want to move, protesting each step, but I forced them to action as I scrambled to his side. He groaned when I rolled him over. He looked like hell, honestly. Beat up and bloodied. Sweaty—and sexy, as always. I wanted to kiss him and hug him and *punch* him for taking such a huge risk for me.

Instead, I just stared down at him, tears welling.

"Stop being such a drama queen," he croaked, and through the haze of my tears I caught him smirking as he reached up and wiped a few tears away. "I'm fine."

His whole body tensed when I hugged him, and his hiss of pain pushed me away.

"Stop moving, you ass," I ordered, my voice thick with emotion. I used what little white magic I had left to treat his injuries. He'd heal on his own, but I owed him a start in easing the pain. Above us, the battle resumed slowly, with crackles of magic cutting through the air like lightning. But I ignored it all, hands roving his battered body and pausing here and there to fuel him with white magic. Darius was my priority—I only wish I'd realized it earlier.

"Kaye," he whispered, but I shook him off, only to look up when he said my name more urgently. Frowning, I glared at him, but then slowly followed his extended arm—right to a pair of demons charging toward us, bodies contorted and movements stiff, like someone had bent them out of shape and tossed them back into the fray.

I turned weakly, ready to defend my dragon to my last breath —when a surge of white magic slammed into the pair and knocked them out of sight. From the shadows and smoke emerged my brother, looking a little worse for the wear but otherwise unharmed.

"Kaye!"

"Where the *fuck* have you been?" I all but shrieked. He jogged toward me and pressed a hard kiss to my forehead.

"Summoning the reinforcements," he told me, chuckling. "These idiots could sleep through any natural disaster, I swear..."

The thunder of charging footsteps sounded through the hive, and supernaturals poured onto every level, finally pushing back Abramelin's men.

"Probably should take that as a sign I need to move the dorms closer to the heart of things," he mused, then gave my shoulder a squeeze. "You okay?"

"Thanks to this guy," I insisted, a hand on Darius's steadily rising and falling chest. My brother grinned.

"I saw that. I owe you the world, dragon, for saving my sister."

Darius shrugged. "You owe me nothing."

"You fight well... for a shifter," my brother teased, and I sat back, rolling my eyes as they clasped hands.

"And you, for a fairy," Darius fired back with a nod toward the pile of shattered demon parts.

"Yes, more to do." With that, my brother stood. "But you will be honored, brother, for what you've done today. For now, I think it's time we get these cretins out of here."

"And when it's all over, we're resuming our conversation," I interjected, pinning them both with the most serious look I could muster—though my heart fluttered at hearing Zayne refer to my dragon as a brother. Darius and Zayne exchanged glances, more unreadable than I would have liked, before my brother disappeared in a burst of fae speed. Sighing, I turned my attentions back to Darius and resumed my healing. While I wanted to appear firm with him, I couldn't wipe the smile from my face.

"Pretty sure you can't yell at me anymore," Darius muttered, wincing when I poked at a healing wound on his chest. "After, you know, my heroic flight—"

"I wouldn't count on that," I told him. "*Both* of you still have a lot of explaining to do."

You know. After the battle was over and an army of creatures that wanted to kill me had been expelled from the hive.

No big deal.

Grimacing, I helped Darius to his feet and moved him out of the way, finding a safe place for us both to ride out the remainder of the battle in peace, our bodies healing and our hearts connecting.

## ❧ 15 ❧

"I HAVE MORE questions than I have answers," I said, as Zayne and I walked along the stone hallway, and crossed the inner courtyard to a wooden door at the back.

"Of course you do," Zayne replied with a smirk, opening the door and stepping inside. I peered into the room curiously, before entering.

*A library.*

The shelves were lined floor-to-ceiling with all kinds of books, from old leather-bound volumes and ledgers, to spell books that looked as though they were hundreds of years old.

"Wow," I breathed, shaking my head in awe.

"This is our history. The elders took great care to preserve as much information as they could over the years. From the origin of the first known fae..." He paused by one of the shelves, his fingers running over a series of books until he found what he was looking for. He pulled it out, flipped open the front page and looked at it intently, as though it held the answers to all the questions of the Universe. "and *your* history...the first known shifter hybrid."

I looked up at him and saw the love he had for me, flickering in the depths of his eyes. In that moment, I knew how hard it had been for him to keep my truth a secret all these years. My heart finally let go of the anger that had been caged, and I felt some of the tension leave my shoulders. I let out a deep breath and accepted the gift he held out to me.

"Thanks, Zayne."

He reached out and placed a hand on my shoulder, squeezing gently for a moment, his eyes shadowed. "I'm sorry I kept this from you, sister."

"I understand why you did. I really do." Tears, sudden and unexpected, pricked my eyes but I blinked them away.

I heard footsteps behind me and when I turned, I saw Darius leaned against the doorway, a curious smile playing on his lips. The look he gave me—the lift of his lips, one raised eyebrow— sent a wave of heat rushing through me.

He held my gaze for a moment before he stepped into the room. When I turned back to Zayne, the look on my brother's face was one of intrigue, as though he could see into my heart, and knew *all* that I felt for Darius.

"I'll leave you two lovebirds alone." He whispered, so that only I could hear.

*Perhaps he could.*

I opened my mouth to tell him that he didn't have to leave, but he waved a hand at me as he walked across the room. "I have a lot to do. Abramelin won't stop until he has destroyed every last clan of shifters. I need to figure out what his next move will be."

"Let us help you," Darius replied, his gray eyes hard, and serious. "Tell us what we can do."

Zayne shook his head, and his gaze dipped downward. "You've done enough for now. Both of you have." He lifted his eyes to Darius, and the expression on his face told me that the two men had formed a bond of mutual respect, and it made my heart sing. "But when we're ready to fight again," he continued, "I expect you both to stand by my side."

"You can count on that," Darius replied, with a hint of a smile.

I watched as Zayne walked out of the room, closing the door behind him. Then my gaze shifted to Darius, who was still standing a few feet away from me.

"So how long have you known?" I asked, narrowing my eyes.

"That you're a shifter?" Something flickered in his eyes then, but it was gone so fast I wondered if I had imagined it.

"*Half* shifter. But yeah, how long?" I folded my arms in front of me. "And don't lie to me."

His eyes darkened a little, but he didn't look away. There was that look again, and this time I identified what it was. *Guilt.*

"Since the night we met."

I felt my eyes widen in disbelief. "Are you serious? You knew I was part shifter since..."

"The cave. Yes...I knew from the moment you walked in."

"But how? "

"It's the same way you can feel the presence of another fairy. We can detect our own kind. We just *feel* it." He shrugged. "I could also sense that you were in danger, which is why I wanted to stay with you." He smiled, and for a minute I was lost in the wicked curve of his lips. "Well, that and because you're absolutely beautiful."

Suddenly, *everything* started to make sense.

I blinked, slightly flustered by the fact that Darius knew so much more about me than I knew about him, and equally as annoyed by the fact that I hadn't even a whisper of a notion that I was anything but fae all my life. How could I have *never* felt that I was somehow different from my fae sisters? Why had I never felt the beast stirring within?

As if reading my mind, Darius spoke. "It's possible that your fae powers were always stronger than your dragon... you know, hidden away, overshadowed by your fae. And perhaps," he paused, and I scowled at him, my eyes flashing. He raised an eyebrow, one corner of his mouth curving up into a smile.

"Perhaps, *what?*"

"Perhaps now your dragon wants to come out and play." His voice had roughened, deepened, his smile going all dark and sexy around the edges.

The challenge in his words caught me off guard. Something had changed in his expression, some of that calm coolness, going out of his eyes, replaced with a burning intensity that I had never seen before. I took a step back, not out of fear, but out of instinct, the same way you'd move if the pitch in a log caught, sending out sparks.

He took a step forward, I took a step back, and felt my back hit a wall. The book was still in my hands and so I held it to my chest, as though it would serve as a barricade between the over-whelming need to be kissed by this dragon, and the untamed desire that burned in his eyes, threatening to be unleashed, should I so much as blink.

Darius took one final step toward me, pulled the book from my hand and set it on the shelf next to us. His lips curved into that cocky grin that sent a rush of heat through my body, and he pulled me against him, his hands roaming over my back, down to my hips.

"You know," One of his hands came up, and he moved my hair aside, and kissed the side of my neck in that sensitive place that sends streaks of fire up your back. His voice rumbled against my throat and I cried out, as I felt his teeth graze my neck. "You really should read that book so you can learn *all* about us dragons...and what happens when we meet our mate."

"What happens?" My words came out as nothing more than a whisper, my breath catching in my throat. "And what do you mean...meet your mate?"

His lips curved into a smile against my skin and it sent a streak of fire up my back. To my frustration, he lifted his head. When he looked at me, his eyes were filled with passion, and a fierceness that took my breath away. "Perhaps it was fate that brought you to me." His words were slow, languid.

His lips came down on mine, cutting off whatever I was going to say. The kiss wasn't rough, but it held the promise of fire, of the animal inside of him just under the surface. His mouth moved over mine, forcefully parting my lips, his tongue sliding into my mouth, slowly, teasing, tempting. Everything inside of me was swirling, riled up, feverish.

Then the kiss deepened, and I wrapped my arms around his shoulders. He was warm and solid, a seemingly immovable rock. Shivers ran down my spine and I felt weightless in his powerful embrace.

One hand slid around my waist, hovering there briefly before moving lower, cupping my ass. His other hand rose to cradle the back of my head, fingers tensing against my hair. It was clear from his movements what was on his mind, and I reluctantly broke the kiss, grinning up at him. The look on his face was one of naked emotion, the longing replaced with love.

"As much as I want to...as much as I want *you*, I have too many questions." It was hard to breathe, like all the oxygen had been burned away with the heat between us. And as much as I had wanted nothing more than to be with him, from the very first night we met, there were now too many unanswered questions about him, his clan, about me...and about us.

He tilted his head to the side and smiled, eyes locked with mine, the intensity of his gaze revealing dark fire, a primal desire. Before I could think of anything more to say, he was kissing me again, this time slowly, *very* slowly.

I lost myself in him, let my hand move to his face, touching his cheek, feeling the rough stubble on his jawline. My hand strayed lower, to the hollow beneath his ear, to his neck. And I felt the beat of his heart under my fingers. Strong...and steady.

His lips moved from my mouth to the hollow beneath my ear. "Take all the time you need. I'm not going anywhere."

The words were whispered against my skin, but they echoed through my mind. Behind my closed eyes, a vision played out. Images of the two of us together, happier than we have ever been, living in a world of unified peace. Then those images were replaced by others, more intense and passionate, invading my senses. Everything else faded into the background, and in that moment, I saw only him and I. My heart swelled with overwhelming hope—of my love for him, and the endless possibilities of our future together.

I heard his sweet, whispered promises, and smiled. I hadn't known this beautiful dragon for long, but already I knew this was just the beginning of something truly magical – something for always.

And while a thousand questions still burned in my mind about what would become of me if my dragon surfaced, I had to trust that for now, his kiss was the only answer I needed.

~

THANK YOU FOR READING **MAGIC FIRE!**
Read book 2...**MAGIC BURN!**

## GET A FREE SEDONA VENEZ BOOK!

https://sedonavenez.com/free-book

# WANT FREE SEDONA VENEZ BOOKS?

Sign up for Sedona Venez's Newsletter and receive FREE BOOKS. In addition to the free stories, you will also get special pricing, exclusive previews and news of new releases.

**GET A FREE SEDONA VENEZ BOOK!**

Join Sedona's mailing list to be the first to know of new releases, free books, special prices and other author giveaways.

https://sedonavenez.com/free-book

# ABOUT THE AUTHOR

USA TODAY BESTSELLING AUTHOR SEDONA VENEZ lives in New York City with her hot ex-military hubby—hooah—and their fur babies. She loves writing sizzling, sexy intricate stories about strong but broken characters who push limits, overcome their fears and risk it all for love.

*Sedona loves to connect with readers!*
www.sedonavenez.com